I0543957

NOW I ACCUSE

GARY BECK SHORT STORIES

Winter Goose
PUBLISHING
where words take flight
wintergoosepublishing.com

This publication is a work of fiction. Names, characters, places, and incidents either are products of the author's imagination or are used fictitiously. This work is protected in full by all applicable copyright laws, as well as by misappropriation, trade secret, unfair competition, and other applicable laws. No part of this book may be reproduced or transmitted in any manner without written permission from Winter Goose Publishing, except in the case of brief quotations embodied in critical articles or reviews. All rights reserved.

Winter Goose Publishing
45 Lafayette Road #114
North Hampton, NH 03862

www.wintergoosepublishing.com
Contact Information: info@wintergoosepublishing.com

Now I Accuse
COPYRIGHT © 2018 by Gary Beck

First Edition, January 2018

Cover Design by Winter Goose Publishing

ISBN: 978-1-941058-75-6

Published in the United States of America

To Jessica,

*On the occasion of your publishing
the tenth book of mine,
I dedicate this collection of short stories to you,
with thanks for your thoughtful, creative,
and passionate commitment to each book*

With love and esteem, Gary

CONTENTS

Now I Accuse 1
Summer Foray 9
Escape To New York 12
The Man Who Shot Stonewall Jackson 24
My Daughter, The Tyrant 29
Pursuit 40
Intrusion 42
The Encounter 59
Varner's Dilemma 63
Extended Meeting 72
Social Agitation 81
The Epidemic Of '53 83
The House In The Stove 94
The Audition 96
Misspent 99
Fearful Flirtation 101
Hippie Brevis 103
Girl Talk 106
Curtain Call 109
In The Garden Trod A Rebel 112
Journey 114
The Iceman 116
Faded Hopes 127
Junkie Interlude 129
An Actor Prepares 131
Losses 134
Assimilation 137
About The Author 140

NOW I ACCUSE

Paris, Oct 1, 2003
Dear Professor Eggert,

I hope your summer on Nantucket was enjoyable and you're back in your history mode at the university. My summer was very productive and I made real progress in the research on my thesis subject: French Republicanism Between the Franco-Prussian War and World War I. Do I dare confess to my doctoral advisor that I sampled the night life of Paris? Well, as much as a poor student could afford.

However, that's not why I'm writing to you. I've discovered a highly unusual document that might have remarkable consequences, if not handled properly. It purports to be a memoir by Alfred Dreyfus, written just prior to his death. I know, I know that you told me Dreyfus was worn out as a thesis subject, but I can't help considering the fact that the Dreyfus Affair became one of the gravest crises of the Third Republic and split the nation into pro- and anti-Dreyfus factions. Yes, I haven't forgotten that you're an authority on the period. I can see the look on your face as you read this and assume that I've strayed from your suggested guidelines. But I've made a unique find! The fantasy come true of every historian.

I was sifting through the archives of the long defunct newspaper L'Aurore, when I found some yellowed, hand written papers in a musty folder. The title page was: "Now I accuse, A.D. Not to be opened until fifty years after my death!" I remembered the famous Zola letter of that title that inflamed France in 1898 and I read on. I hope I've whetted your curiosity by now, but if I haven't yet, the following statement will. In this old document, Dreyfus accuses the French Army of the murder of Emile Zola! That's right, Professor, murder. Is this starting to sound like the plot of a mystery novel?

Forgive me if I seem to be rambling on so much, but as you can imagine this find awakened my enthusiasm. I left out much of the description of his early misfortunes, because I know you're familiar with them. I believe that the following excerpts from the memoir will arouse your interest and I eagerly look forward to your response. Let's avoid electronic communication, because this could turn out to be a volatile subject, so no telephone or e-mail. If I appear to be overly cautious, please suspend judgment until you read the material for yourself.

July 10, 1935

It is with great reluctance that I set pen to paper and write this indictment just a few days before Bastille Day, the holiday that symbolizes liberty, of an institution that I once served with honor, the Army of France. I was still an overage captain in 1894, slow to get promotion mostly due to anti-Semitic resentment that permeated the General Staff. Yet there were a few officers who saw me as a man, not just a Jew who was intruding in the officer corps. This acceptance from men of tolerance allowed me to pursue my duties with integrity, secure of my place in the service of my country.

Then that infamous day that shattered my life and the lives of my beloved family forever. Without any inkling of the conspiracy that had been developing towards me, I was arrested and accused of passing secrets to the Germans. I was convicted of treason by a military tribunal in a nightmarish court martial that throughout felt as if it were happening to someone else. Then, in what became the most agonizing day of my life, the Army I revered paraded me in front of my brother officers at the École Militaire. With the contemptuous eyes of everyone on me, they ritually tore off my badges of rank and insignia. A staff officer, immaculate in his dress uniform, broke my sword across his knee. After several days in a military prison, spit on by my guards, they shipped me to that hellhole in the South Atlantic, Devil's Island.

Of course, like all Frenchmen, I knew of Devil's Island. But if it was ever mentioned publicly, it was either with contempt or indifference for the luckless devils sent there. There I was, having served France loyally and honorably, condemned to life imprisonment in that remote penal colony. During my first year of agony I thought often of my beloved country's motto: Liberté, Égalité, Fraternité. Well, the General Staff stole my liberté, but I found more égalité and fraternité on that monstrous island in the company of those poor rejects from France, then I ever felt among my fellow officers. My daily suffering was the more tormenting because of my complete innocence.

My beloved wife and brother never ceased their efforts on my behalf. And lo and behold, after four terrible years, they procured a new trial for me. Hope soared in my breast. Surely my country would realize that it had misjudged a loyal Frenchman. But then despair. Once again the court martial found me guilty and I was returned to Devil's Island. This time even the pledges of my family to never give up their efforts to free me could not sustain my battered spirit. I do not know how I endured the inflictions that fate had decreed for me.

Then events that I only learned about later took control of my destiny. One of France's greatest writers, Emile Zola, became interested in my case. He learned some facts about forged evidence and certain officers who lied about me that established my innocence. In an act of great moral courage, M. Zola defied the might of the French Army and in 1898 accused the General Staff of falsely convicting me. This stirred up a hornet's nest that divided the country into two opposing factions; one that believed me innocent; the other guilty. Passions were so incensed that some newspaper editors speculated that the nation might come to civil war.

Then miracle of miracles. I was rescued from hell and brought back to France in 1900 and pardoned by the President of the Republic, M. Loubert. I was quietly restored to duty and even promoted to major. Has any subaltern ever had to go through so much to be promoted? I owed my freedom and possible good future all to my beloved wife and brother, and the conscience of that great man, M. Zola. I thanked him repeatedly for saving my life, but he modestly dismissed my eternal gratitude and refused any money offered by my brother.

It is with heavy heart that I now charge that the death of that light of France, M. Zola, on September 29, 1902, at the age of sixty-two, was no accident as reported in the press. The story given out was that he was found dead of asphyxiation in his sealed apartment, victim of a defective fireplace flue. I went to his funeral with a depth of sorrow that I still feel to this day as my death approaches, for the noble benefactor who saved my life. Afterwards, I tried to ignore some of my fellow officers, who gloated that the meddler had been punished for his insult to the Army. I only learned the horrible truth four years later.

On July 21, 1906, the Court of Appeals annulled my guilty verdict and I was promoted to Lieutenant Colonel. At the same place of my shame twelve years earlier, when I was broken in front of the officer corps at the École Militaire, I was awarded the Legion of Honor. It seemed for a brief moment that I had regained my life. But then, as I paraded proudly in front of my brother officers, a voice called from the anonymous ranks: "When your notoriety dies down, Dreyfus, we'll get you, just like we got Zola."

I managed to get through the rest of the ceremony without revealing the horror that possessed me. That night, while everyone else was asleep, I sat in my study and considered what I should do. I had no doubt that I owed my life to M. Zola, a debt that now could never be repaid. The more I thought about the murder of that great man, the more my outrage grew. A terrible crime had been committed and only the murderers and I knew about it. I was obligated to do something. But what? There was no one in the Army I could trust, so my only possible ally was the press. Would that brave editor of L'Aurore champion the dead on hearsay? And what would happen to my beloved family if I accused the Army of murder?

After many hours of painful and confused thought, I concluded that it would be too great a risk for my family if I went public with my accusation. I could not help feeling like a coward about my decision and I thought of ending my life with my service revolver, which had never been fired in battle. Then the thought of the harm my suicide would do to my beloved family persuaded me to renounce the only escape that would allow me to retain my honor. So I went to work each day at the War Ministry and came home each evening to my beloved family, but inside I was a hollow man. I was a hostage for my family's continued safety and well-being.

After that day I became much more wary of everyone, especially my fellow officers, and I was suspicious of everything that happened around me. My beloved wife assumed it was due to my suffering on Devil's Island and I could not confide the truth to her. Two years went by with me in a highly nervous state. I began to think I was imagining threats where there were none. But then a frightening incident occurred at M. Zola's bier on June 4, 1908. I frequently went to that great man's bier to pay my respects and silently thank him for saving me, as well as to apologize for not avenging him. That day, a petty journalist, a military correspondent, a toady for the Army, pulled out a pistol and yelled, "Zola and Dreyfus have defiled France," and shot me.

Fortunately, the wounds were not serious and my assailant was quickly apprehended by the police. Not unexpectedly, he never came to trial and was released several weeks later. It was obvious that I was still in danger and my family might be also. Soon after, I retired from the Army, disillusioned with the institution that I had tried to serve with honor, which in return had betrayed, reviled, and abused me. We lived quietly in seclusion, avoiding any publicity that might lead my enemies to us. I went through the outward motions of a paterfamilias, while inside I smoldered with guilt, frustration, and impotent rage.

Then once again the Germans invaded France. Despite my decrepit age of fifty-five, I saw a last chance to redeem what I considered to be my still tarnished honor in the service of my country. My beloved wife was bitterly opposed to my reenlistment in the Army that had so cruelly betrayed me. It took a while to persuade her that I owed my allegiance and duty to France, despite the anti-Semitic persecution I had endured from so many of my fellow countrymen.

I fought at Verdun, where so many brave Frenchmen sacrificed their lives for the Republic. And I never said one word in public against the generals, who callously expended our national treasure, an entire generation of our youth. My beloved son Pierre died in the trenches, as did my beloved brother's son, along with the legions of the young. Many of the men who conspired to destroy my life perished in the Great War. There was one ironic death, Colonel von Schwartzkoppen, the German military attaché who intrigued with that treacherous villain, Esterhazy, the real spy. On his deathbed on the eastern front, he cried out, "People of France, hear me! Dreyfus is innocent."

My last testimony is almost complete. I have experienced terrible suffering in my lifetime, perhaps more than most men. Yet I will not die embittered thanks to the love of my life, my beloved wife, Lucie. However, hatred still poisons our land and once again the Army prepares to consume our youth in the mad quest for glory. I can do nothing more for my beloved country, except go to my grave with the undimmed hope that sanity may yet prevail and good men will appear and guide the nation with justice and honor. I attest that everything I have written is, to the best of my knowledge, true. Long Live France.

Well, Professor, what do you think? I left out various sections, but this should give you the gist of the document. Am I right? Is it a find? At first I thought it was wishful thinking on my part. Then I went on the all-pervasive Web and discovered some interesting information. In 1972, the city council of Rennes, where the second Dreyfus trial took place, refused to dedicate a high school to Dreyfus. In 1985, the Army refused to allow a statue of Dreyfus to be installed in the École Militaire, where his degradation took place in 1895.

Am I rambling on too much, Professor? By now you should be able to tell how excited I am by what might not prove to be just musty material. To demonstrate that the Dreyfus Affair still is timely, the Army didn't officially pardon Dreyfus until 1995! Then a general admitted that the case was a military conspiracy and an innocent man was condemned by false evidence.

Now you have a basic outline of the memoir and related events up to quite recently, so it is time to present the crucial issue. If I pursue this subject, I will, in effect, accuse the French Army of the murder of M. Zola, as claimed by Dreyfus. After all, that is what his historic document represents, an allegation of a conspiratorial homicide. I have no corroborating evidence, no witnesses, and no other information, which means a research project to attempt to discover further material. Would you approve this effort?

There is one other consideration that is disturbing me. Obviously, the French Army is still highly sensitive about their part in the Dryfus Affair, even though it happened more than a hundred years ago. How will they react if I accuse them of murder? Will they assume my activities are scholarly excursions into the past, with no implications today? As you have repeatedly told me, the French are a peculiar people, with extreme passions and prejudices that are sometimes difficult for a foreigner to understand. What if the French Army feels threatened by my discovery? Would they conceivably arrange an accident for me? . . . I interrupted this letter to check the flue in my fireplace to verify that it was drawing properly. Ha, ha. An academic's weak joke.

Seriously, Professor Eggert. I'm not the bravest of individuals. And I surely don't want to risk my life for what might turn out to be a piece of historical trivia. Yet I know it's the duty of the historian to reclaim the past honestly, for the benefit of future scholars. Is a historian supposed to have a code of honor? So. Would my work create an incident? Am I being paranoid? Am I creating a delusional fantasy to enhance my worth? Is the French Army still capable of malevolent acts? I urgently require your advice. Please respond immediately.

Respectfully, your student at-risk,
Vincent

SUMMER FORAY

In summertime the slums are ripe with yelling, fighting, running, playing children, whose parents can't afford to send them to camp. Groups of thin, undernourished, underloved and dirty children riotously course the streets, investigating every piece of discarded refuse, rifling sundry garbage cans in search of alluring treasures, wading through slimy and befouled puddles of undrained water, stagnating in the torpid fetid streets. They can be known simply by listening, since most of these children do everything as loudly as possible.

The sound levels related to slum children's activities are numerous and diverse. They range from a mother's indignant shrieks of fatal injuries done to a hapless and bewildered urchin on whom the pack turned, to lustily bellowed directions to participants in a stickball game. But the most dreadful sound is the agonizing protest screech of brakes, when drivers barely miss some careless, reckless child. Then there is a veritable deluge of imprecation directed at the boy who did not look, before galloping blindly into the gutter.

The fortunate children, bathing suited and full of curses, run screaming under the spray of open fire hydrants. The older children control the flow with their hands, turning powerful jets on the buses. When a bus is caught unaware, the frantic yells and attempts of the drenched passengers to close the windows brings loud squeals of delight to the children, who take flight before vengeance can descend. They leave their elders sitting on the stoops and leaning from windows, to enjoy the chaos. This was my first real glimpse of the lower east side.

I had arranged to sublet an apartment on East 14th Street for July and August. Since the rent was only forty dollars a month, this was years before gentrification, I wasn't too particular about the neighborhood. All I could tell about the area was that the buildings were ancient and decaying. I had only seen the apartment at night for a few moments. It was a railroad flat with a bathtub in the kitchen. The toilet was in a tiny room in the hall, shared by the other tenants on the floor. The surroundings were so novel to me that instead of seeing it as a squalid roach-infested firetrap, I felt the beginnings of my first adventure away from home.

I didn't have a phone yet and I had to make some calls, so I went down five flights of stairs to the dingy bar downstairs. I could barely see when I went inside. One naked light bulb burned, swinging back and forth on a furry, fraying cord. It cast eerie shadows twisting on the walls in a solemn ritual that reflected on the sawdust floor. The faint light dimly lit the length of the gloomy, ancient bar, casting a feeble glow on an old, weather-beaten bartender talking baseball to a barfly. A sodden woman sat hunched and mumbling at a beer-stained table.

The bar occupied the ground floor of the crumbling tenement. I discovered by reading the mailboxes that it was overflowing with Poles and Puerto Ricans. The ghostly room could have been hacked from a razed forest, with stumps of people as the only surviving witnesses to the blaze. Save for the whiskey and beer signs, the layers of dirt, and the almost fossilized people, all that was noticeable was a large-screen television broadcasting a baseball game. A prominent sign over the cash register warned: "Credit is for Heaven. Pay now." The desiccated barkeep stood guard behind the scarred and cigarette-burned bar. "Do you have a pay phone?" I asked politely. He stared at me blankly. "Téléphono, por favor?" I tried. No response. I mimed dialing and said slowly: "Tel-a-phone?" He shrugged and pointed to the back of the room.

With misgivings that I might be entering an astral black hole, I cautiously made my way through the dark room, wondering what could be lurking in the back. After careful groping, guiding myself by running my hand along the greasy wall, I found the phone. It was situated between the aromatic bathrooms and I breathed through my mouth to endure the odor. I made my calls as quickly as I could, then fumbled my way to the front door, where I didn't pause, saying "Thank you" over my shoulder to the indifferent bartender.

Once safely outside, I took a deep breath, relieved to have survived the foray into the stygian depths. I climbed the five flights to reach my new home on the top floor, legs aching from the ascent, chest panting from the altitude. I unlocked the apartment door and reached for the light switch. I heard a faint, scurrying sound and the sudden illumination highlighted dozens of cockroaches, fleeing for cover. The flaws in my tenement paradise were rapidly revealing themselves, but the feeling of not being answerable to anyone was intoxicating. I went to bed, still exhilarated from the heady feeling of being alone in my own place. As I was falling asleep, my last thought was that I'd check out my new neighborhood in the morning.

ESCAPE TO NEW YORK

Well, life had definitely taken a turn for the better. I still had my job teaching acting at Gotham University's School of the Arts. This meant that I could afford to keep my East Village apartment. This, of course, was not good news for my landlord, a slumlord who retained his property long enough to strike gold when the neighborhood became gentrified. Now I wouldn't have to slink in and out of the building, avoiding his acqusitional fingers, and he would have to find a different way to get rid of me. I also might have a new girlfriend, Anitra Blavatsky, a flighty artist who I met at an opening at a trendy gallery in Chelsea. When she told me her name I guess I didn't react properly, so she informed me haughtily that she was a lineal descendant of Madame Blavatsky, the famous spiritualist and mystic. This meant nothing to me, so I casually commented, "That's nice. Did she tell fortunes?" Anitra thought I was being clever and laughed at my wit. She was tall, bony, and handsome in a chilly sort of way that I found appealing. She was generally out of town assisting a famous artist, whose art consisted of wrapping buildings or other things in plastic, so we talked a lot on the phone.

    I don't know if fate owed me an upswing, but life hadn't been easy for the last two years. I came to New York to escape the constraints of my Boston upbringing. I was the second son in a long family line that had a rigid tradition: the first son became a doctor; the second son became a lawyer. The allure of the law was nonexistent to me, so my choice was simple: obey the family dicta and live oppressed, or refuse history's mandate and suffer the consequences. When I chose to study theater at Northeastern, instead of pre-law at Harvard, Mum and Dad brought in the

Gurkhas to suppress rebellion. Uncles inveighed, aunts entreated, cousins reasoned, Mum pouted and Dad fumed. When their combined efforts failed to daunt me, Dad trundled out the heavy brigade, Granddad doctor Arthur Hayes Kensington, IV. Fourth, as he was respectfully referred to, rarely emerged from the glacial isolation of his den, where he cackled over illustrated Moliere plays that satirized his profession. His mobilization indicated that the front-line troops were faltering.

I may have been outnumbered, but I wasn't outgunned, and I resisted every assault until my funds were expended. Then the family issued the final ultimatum: unconditional surrender, or exile. With a light heart, a lighter wallet, and lightest of all, the freedom of release from an unwanted burden, I entrained for New York City and moved into a cheap hotel on upper Broadway. I quickly got an acting job in an off-off Broadway theater company, unpaid of course. I earned a living performing as a silent clown at 72nd Street and Central Park West. The park habitués enjoyed my act, which I concluded by making balloon animals for the kiddies. Single and five-dollar bills flowed into my baseball cap begging bowl and I was soon able to afford an apartment of my own. An actor acquaintance relocated to Hollywood and I inherited his apartment on East Ninth Street between Avenues B and C, where the yuppie invasion hadn't penetrated too deeply yet. I transferred my clown act to Saint Mark's Place and Second Avenue, a short stroll from home, and it prospered. At lease-renewal time I signed my name to the precious document, sent it off hoping for the best and behold, it came back with the landlord's signature. I was a genuine New Yorker.

It didn't take long for the landlord to discover his mistake and descend upon my peaceful domicile with unmitigated wrath. When he finally stopped bellowing like an anguished steer, I tried to reason with him, but he wouldn't listen. The implacable gouger of the poor had planned to rent my apartment to a yuppie pioneer who would be willing to endure the loneliness of the urban frontier and pay exorbitantly, until other settlers arrived. He rantingly demanded that I vacate the apartment. I loftily refused. War was declared and I was summoned to housing court. Judge Evictus, no doubt marooned on this ignoble bench since the dethronement of political boss Carmine DeSapio, was more resentful of tenants than landlords. But I had a signed lease, a legally executed document that entitled me to the apartment. However much they conspired and connived against me, I wasn't budging. Finally, despairing of another solution the judge advised the landlord to offer me money to vacate the premises. The pusillanimous landlord offered seven hundred dollars, one month's rent, and I courteously refused. Judge Evictus, out of options, glared malevolently at me and begrudgingly dismissed the case.

When I got outside, the intoxicating air of victory filled my lungs, but was immediately superseded by city carcinogens. As I scaled down my respiratory ambitions, the landlord accosted me and swore unrelenting war, unless I departed. I sneered at his threat, but made a mental note to visit the library and review tenant's rights. I knew he couldn't cut off heat and hot water to my sixth-floor aerie, since some of the tenants in the partially gentrified building were yuppies, and they wouldn't tolerate the loss of creature comforts. I spent some time speculating what the landlord could do to me, but aside from wild fantasies of sponsored break-ins, or assassination, I didn't see how he could dislodge me. A wave of well-being surged through me. I had a secure apartment for two years, as long as I could pay the rent. A celebration was called for, but I had no one to share my elation. Anitra was out of the country, learning to wrap the Mosque of Omar in plastic, as long as the faithful didn't stone the unbelievers for profaning a holy place. I couldn't understand how wrapping something made by man or nature in plastic could be art, when any deli counterman could do that.

I originally thought I wanted to be a theater director, but the endless struggle to impose one's will on the production quickly made it lose its luster. I was anything but a control freak. The ongoing prospect of trying for quality performances from a mixed talent base of off-off Broadway actors led me to playwriting. I enjoyed acting. I wasn't driven to build my career in the lust to be adored, the primary need of most actors. I just loved performing in front of an audience. My clown show allowed me complete freedom and also supported me. So I started my first play, a grandiose three act family tragedy. It took me a while to realize that my play lacked certain ingredients: a theme, a plot, a dramatic structure. Despite these critical oversights, there was some good dialogue, mostly filial invective against a domineering father that sounded suspiciously autobiographical. So I put the play aside and started something simpler: a one act, two-character play about a young couple falling out of love.

I was painfully familiar with falling out of love. My last girlfriend, Ellen Markson, had broken up with me for cause. She objected to my rampant display of lust. It's not that she didn't enjoy sex, but it had to be part of a larger relationship. Ellen was a law student and wanted to debate the issues she encountered in class. Marbury versus Madison was low on my priority list, compared to diddlying Ellen's taut, slightly hypertense, sexy little body. In a last effort to stabilize the fraying fabric of our relationship, Ellen suggested we follow an agenda: dinner, discussions, sex. I excelled in two out of three, but Ellen demanded all of them. I fell asleep during the thrilling climax of Brown versus the Board of Education and inexcusably violated the covenant. Ellen gathered the few items she kept at my apartment, a hair brush, a tooth brush, clean panties, deodorant, and abandoned me for the niceties of the law. I berated myself for weeks for losing her. I could have mastered the art of looking interested and nodding my head periodically like a dipping bird. Actors and politicians did that all the time.

So on I wrote and waited for the light and had just enough meat and bread, and didn't care who put a bullet in his head. But in a thunderbolt of revelation, I saw that I needed a theater. After all, what good is a play without a theater? The off-off Broadway company that I had worked with as an actor specialized in updated versions of the classics. I had appeared in Richard III, set in the Chicago stockyards; Prometheus Bound, set in the American embassy in Tehran; Hamlet, set in a mental institution. The last venture almost prepared me for institutionalization. I played Horatio, Hamlet's loyal friend and confidante. My function, in this director's psychotic exercise, was to give Hamlet a swig of Thorazine whenever he faced a crisis. Not even the most faithful friends or devoted families could sit through this atrocity. When this not too solid run ended, I left the company without a single sarcastic remark about the show. After all, by being there I was as guilty as everyone else who participated in this decomposition, or as the deluded director preferred, deconstruction of a classic.

With a one act play in hand I approached various small theaters and a pattern of rejection quickly emerged: "We'll get back to you if we're interested." "Join our playwrights workshop, for a substantial fee, and you'll get a reading, someday." "No unsolicited scripts." "Agent submissions only." The search for new talent was obviously a myth. I briefly considered joining a workshop, but the thought of sitting with other playwrights and wagging for recognition was a dismal prospect. It's not that I was unprepared for the possibility of rejection, but the discovery that theater was a restricted community was unsettling. Anitra had already lectured me at length on the need to network, but the combination of her know-it-all attitude and my inherent stubbornness made me dismiss her advice. She was always giving me useless advice in a smug, self-satisfied voice that would raise my hackles. The coincidence that this one time she might be right was irritating and provoked me to childish resistance. I had no desire to become social, or political, so perhaps a career as a playwright wasn't optimum at the moment.

I loved performing for a live audience. I was getting more and more involved in playwriting. I was somewhat of a loner, an anomaly in theater, which had herd-like characteristics. One possibility that occurred to me was to write a one man show that I could perform outdoors. If the results were worthwhile, I could raise money, rent a theater and produce the show myself. The more I thought about it, the more excited I became. All I had to do was write a show. I could do that. I also had to learn about producing, so I went online and found an enormous amount of information. My printer was down, so I just browsed the web, scanning the huge, undigested mass of data that was mostly personal revelation by the inept, rather than how-to info. Then I visited the Tompkins Square library on East 10th Street, between Avenues A and B, and found a very useful book: *How to Produce for the Small Theater.* I also noticed a lot of attractive young women and made an instant decision to use the public library more often.

The book was very informative, once you waded through the usual artistic camouflage. The two revelations that really shook me up were how expensive everything was, and how many people you needed to do it: director, producer, stage manager, production manager, technical director, designers, techs, stagehands, house manager, box office, ushers. If the book was right, you needed a small army just to produce a play off-off Broadway. I had one or two theater friends who might help me, but for the rest I'd have to hire strangers, not the most reassuring prospect. I tried to eliminate some of the personnel, but the best I could come up with was for me to be the producer/director, as well as the entire cast. It looked like I needed all the others. Then I reviewed the budget: theater rental, lighting equipment, construction supplies, personnel, advertising and promotion. The list went on and on, indicating that art wasn't cheap. I went over the sample budget several times and the only thing I could eliminate was advertising and promotion, if I didn't require an audience. I couldn't find any satisfactory answers, so I gave up and went home.

Before I could shift from dejected brooding to clinical depression, Anitra phoned from Germany to update me on the progress of the wrapping project. The faithful had objected to desecration of Allah's house on earth, so now they were aspiring to wrap the Kremlin in plastic. My suggestion that they wrap trouble spots around the world, like Kosovo, or Rwanda, thus giving the warring factions time to cool off, wasn't appreciated. After a lengthy silence, I told her that I was thinking about producing a one man show off-off Broadway, but it required a lot of money. She rambled on for a few minutes about how the monthly United States trade deficit of 30 billion dollars was a military/industrial conspiracy to make foreign countries dependent on our purchases. Then we'd suddenly stop buying and watch their economies collapse from over-production. When I asked what that had to do with my wanting to produce a play, she replied, "Isn't it obvious?" and hung up.

I must confess that I really didn't understand Anitra at all. She was proud of assisting Sophisto, the nickname I had given her master of plastic, but I was a retrograde and preferred paper. Her personal artistic work was putting miniature images of Buckminster Fuller's geodesic dome, which she claimed was the greatest invention since the wheel, on coins. She affixed mini-domes on nickels, dimes, and quarters, each a different shade of green. Fortunately, when she first told me, I didn't make a flip remark like, "It sounds like small change to me." So instead of alienating her instantly with my boorish ways, she had taken charge of my cultural education. I wanted to take charge of her body, but she kept me at a distance, frostily chiding me: "You must learn to control your low physical appetites and aspire to a higher plane of existence." I risked a quip: "I'll fly the SST next time I travel," that met with distant disapproval. I couldn't figure out why what I considered normal sex urges were so unacceptable to so many women.

It was clear that it wasn't practical for me to produce my own one man show, given my current economic condition. I guesstimated that a three-week run would cost twenty thousand dollars. If I really skimped for the next twenty years, and if there was no inflation or currency devaluation, I could probably afford to produce the show in 2021. Considering the present level of decadence, theater might be obsolete by then, except for mega-musicals and shockers. Fewer and fewer people were willing to make the requisite effort to think about theater. If serious theater disappeared because it was easier to passively spectate musicals, movies, and TV, that would be frightening for our culture. We were being mind wiped at an increasingly dangerous rate. Too many generations of children have been planted in front of the TV by parents, instead of being nurtured. If you could erase the thought process with electronics, I guess you could wrap things in plastic and call it art.

So my brief career as a producer was over before it even started. I didn't know if it was worth my time and effort to write a one man show and perform it on the street, if I couldn't bring it to a theater. Instead, I renewed my commitment to my acting students at Gotham U.'s School of the Arts. My initial enthusiasm had slowly faded, as I tried to motivate them to risk emotional extremes in search of actor's expression. But they were bred on sitcoms. The safe and simplistic acting methods of TV had become ingrained in their plodding creation of characters. It's ironic that actors were once the despised rejects of a class society and clawed their way out of the gutter with their talent. Now they all went to college, where they learned a little bit about acting, then were welcomed into the middle-class society that once looked down on them. It's weird how going to college can legitimize what was once a low-life profession.

My silent clown street show was the redeeming creative factor in what was becoming a comfortable life. There was no fourth wall on the street. The artificial contrivance that separated fearful actors from their audience was inconceivable, if you wanted to reach people on the street. If they couldn't feel you in a reassuring way, they just wouldn't respond. Our streets were already overwhelmed by the representatives of decay: junkies, drug dealers, muggers, mentally ill homeless, criminals of all sorts, and an endless stream of stressed citizens, building frustration and rage, only waiting for a target. I attracted all types when I was performing. Some types of psychos were threatened by a silent clown and I had to be very careful to avoid an emotional eruption that could get unpleasant. Other people, demented or retarded, reacted with childish demands for attention. Low-lifes heckled, or interrupted the show, and this was no longer an age when spectators told them to shut up. The growing number of difficulties in performing on St. Mark's Place impelled me to return to my safe old site at 72nd Street and Central Park West.

I was very lucky. No one had replaced me at the park entrance, where I had pioneered a lucrative site. If someone occupied the spot, I couldn't consider them a claim jumper and reach for my six shooter. After all, I had abandoned the mother lode. But I was back, my audience was glad to see me, and the money flowed in. I averaged about fifty dollars per ten-minute show, including another ten minutes making balloon animals. I usually did three shows in an hour and a half. Balloons, make-up, and carfare cost me about fifteen dollars a day, so I was doing pretty well. I could reasonably hope to perform into November, maybe even later, if global warming persisted. I could start again in March, again depending on climate conditions. So for eight months, I could do my show Friday, Saturday, and Sunday mornings, between ten a.m. and noon, weather permitting. I taught two acting classes at Gotham U. on Monday and Wednesday mornings, so my afternoons and evenings were free.

I did some basic arithmetic regarding my income and concluded that I could easily save two hundred dollars per week, barring a calamity. If all went according to plan, I would have enough money to produce my one man show in two years or so. That didn't seem outlandishly long. It would take three or four months to write the first draft and a few more months for revisions. Then it would take two or three months to learn the show and create the personal touches that would make it interesting. I'd want to perform the show for a while, say three or four months, then revise it and perform it again, which could take another six months. I was now up to a year and a half of working on the show before formal production.

The plan was actually beginning to seem realistic and I got a tremendous rush of exhilaration, because I had never planned anything more than a few days ahead in my entire life. I desperately wanted to share my feelings of satisfaction, but I didn't have any close friends and my family would have said something negative. So I had lots of exuberance bottled inside and it made me much more benevolent towards my acting students, a group that usually feared my caustic tongue. When Anitra called from Paris to rhapsodize about Sophisto's latest wrapping project, the Eiffel Tower, I didn't respond with proper enthusiasm. I could almost feel the sudden drop in temperature when I quipped, "Maybe you should consider wrapping Mont Blanc." There was a frigid silence, then she replied coldly, "I don't expect you to understand the significance of conceptual art, but you could at least keep your unenlightened comments to yourself. Perhaps you should get a dog. He might appreciate your immature sense of humor."

It was becoming clear that Anitra and I were not meant to be, for we operated on two entirely different wavelengths. When it came to art, she was UHF and I wasn't even VHF. My faint hope that a stable sexual relationship would bind us together was obviously misplaced. We couldn't even get beyond Basic Bickering 101. I ignored her suggestion of a dog and apologized for my insensitivity. I felt like a hypocrite, because my ulterior motive was to have sex with her, although it was a dimming prospect. We chatted about neutral topics for a while, then I told her about my newly revised plan to produce my one man show. After a dubious silence, Anitra haughtily corrected my political incorrectness: "The proper way to describe your project would be to call it a one person show." I guess I was impatient. "Okay. It's a one person show. What do you think of the idea?" Her reply was indifferent. "It sounds a bit asocial to me."

I hung up before I said anything out of anger, but I was simmering. I don't know what I expected from her, but in the least I anticipated some kind of encouragement. That was probably unreasonable, since I was usually sarcastic about her work. Why should she be more generous than I was? However, my need for approval was great and I reacted to her abrupt dismissal of my plan with extreme disappointment. In fact, I found myself thinking that we weren't really suited to each other at all, and her body wasn't that appealing. Besides, she was hardly ever in New York City. When she was, she still seemed to be wrapped in plastic. I didn't have to work very hard to justify sour grapes. Maybe Anitra and I could be friends, only time would tell, but we wouldn't be lovers. That wasn't too difficult to decide, since we never got to be lovers in the first place.

I resolved to go ahead with my plan to produce a one man show—so there, Anitra—and I immediately started a production list of what I needed to do. I also pledged to rededicate my energies to my acting students and not be so critical of their efforts, however paltry I felt them to be. I never told them that I performed as a silent clown and I briefly wondered how they would react if they learned about it. Probably with disdain, I concluded, since it wasn't neat, safe, or antiseptic. Well, I had no intention of telling them. I could imagine the scorn that "Ernest the Emoter," the theater department chairman, might heap on me. If he discovered that I was a common street performer he was pompous enough to think that my extracurricular activities wouldn't enhance Gotham U. So I would continue to maintain the grease paint wall of silence about my clown show. Once I dismissed my concern with Ernest, I started thinking about all the pretty girls I might meet at an internet café. It was too late to go out, but I had something to look forward to tomorrow.

THE MAN WHO SHOT STONEWALL JACKSON

It happened once before, when I was a young man. The newspapers clamored for war, self-appointed know-it-alls told us why we had to fight and everyone believed them, especially the youngsters like me who got all fired up to join the army. So now, when those big headlines screamed "Remember The Maine," there wasn't any more doubt that there would be war with Spain. And off they went to enlist, just like they were going to a picnic, as irreverent and ignorant as we were back in 1861. My eldest son told me he had to join up and I tried to discourage him. I told him how crazy it was for two groups of men to stand and blaze away at each other, but he wouldn't listen. All he said was, "War's not fought that way anymore, Pa."

So I held my peace and watched him go, like my pa watched me go. When he died of yellow fever, before he even fought in a battle, it was another terrible affliction that I had to accept. But I guess he was right about it being a new kind of war, because it was over pretty quick and we got all these new places; Cuba, Puerto Rico, The Philippines, and Guam. I never even heard of Guam. So I kept on farming and doing my chores but I was pretty much empty inside. I had been that way ever since the surrender at Appomattox, which ended my daily suffering, but left me a hollow man. I went through all the motions of the living and tried my best to be a good husband and father, and I never told anyone how I felt. How could anyone who hadn't been there understand? Sometimes, when I went to town and saw the few old hands who survived the entire war, like me, there was nothing we could say. We just looked at each other for a moment, nodded in recognition that we were still alive, and moved on.

Then one day, long after Spain surrendered, I saw a soldier who had just come home from the Philippines. I was buying something in Dahlgren's general store and his pa brought him in. He had that look that I hadn't seen since the war with the Yankees. His flesh was sagging on his bones and his uniform hung on him like a scarecrow on a hard luck farm. He walked as if it was a great effort to put one foot after the other. Old Mr. Dahlgren kept prodding him to tell us what it was like over there, but he refused to talk, until his pa urged him. Then he looked at everyone for a moment and said coldly: "You want to know what it was like? I'll tell you. I watched my buddies die in ambushes, or of tropical diseases, or in battles with savages who just kept coming at us, even after we shot them. I watched my friends butcher women and children!" A look of absolute horror ate his face. "All I saw was death and suffering. Is that what you wanted to hear?" Then he turned and walked out. I couldn't get him out of my mind the rest of the day.

That night I thought about the war with the Yankees, which I had shut out of my life a long time ago. I remembered how I had rushed to join up that spring of 1861. I ignored Pa when he told me not to go, just like my boy ignored me. Then Pa told me how bad it was when he fought the Mexicans in '46, but I didn't believe him. Everyone I knew was hurrying to the colors and I wasn't about to be last. We were going to whip the Yankees good, then go back home with our chests full of medals. Once I was in uniform it didn't take long for me to wake up. Almost half the boys I joined up with got killed or wounded in our first battle at Manassas. Maybe the Yankees finally ran off as fast as they could for Washington DC, but not before they put up a mighty good fight. We fought up and down Virginia for the next two years and got leaner, hungrier, tireder, and sicker. The more we ran out of ammunition, food, or shoes, the more the Yankees kept coming. We learned everything about the horror of soldiering the hard way.

One day we were camped somewhere near Chancellorsville, after a tough battle where we whipped the Yankees good. Of course it wasn't like when the war first started. Then we knew we were better men than the city folk and immigrants they were going to send against us. Before First Manassas, most of us talked about beating them proper, then going home. If anyone thought it would go on and on for years, they didn't say it where I heard. Anyhow, we had been resting because it had been a long, hard fight and these Yankees weren't like the rabbits who used to run when they were beaten. When these Yankees lost, they retreated resentfully and we knew they'd be back. Then the word raced through the camp. Stonewall was dead. Rumors, like disease, travel swiftly in an army, especially when it's bad news. This hit me and the old hands particularly hard, because we were the 31st Virginia and we were Stonewall's men from the beginning.

We rushed to Colonel Barstow's tent, but he didn't know any more than we did. Messengers kept arriving, each one with different news. The only thing they all agreed on was that Stonewall had been shot. The colonel finally got tired of our pushing and shoving at the messengers and he sent us back to our bivouac area. But he promised to let our company commander, Lieutenant Rambeau, know as soon as he learned anything. We thanked the colonel, who was one of only three officers left in the regiment who had been with us from the start. All the others had been killed or invalided out. Colonel Barstow had started as a young lieutenant, full of fire and noble speeches. Now he was as old and tired as the rest of us. We snickered about Lieutenant Rambeau as we walked. He was a momma's boy, a blond-haired stringbean with a mushy face that always looked ready to cry. He had reported to the regiment a few days ago, but he disappeared somehow before the fighting started. The joke going around the camp was who would shoot him first, us or them. Soldiers deserted other regiments before a fight, but not in the 31st Virginia.

We waited for news, but didn't relax much. A couple of the younger boys babbled about beating the Yankees again, but the old hands quickly shut them up. By now we knew we could beat them and beat them, but they would still keep coming. We were sick, tired, cold, and hungry, and we didn't have much hope left. The gossip around the campfire was no longer about victory. A few diehards still kept trying to convince the rest of us that massa Robert and ole Stonewall would find a way to defeat the Yankees. Most of us didn't buy it. Now Stonewall was dead. One of the kids asked what would happen if General Lee got killed, but an old hand kicked him a few times and the kid slunk off, leaving the rest of us to brood about things. I couldn't help thinking how lucky that kid was to get off so lightly. We had just lost our father and that dumb kid was talking about losing our grandfather. We didn't need any more bad luck.

Later that night we found out that Stonewall wasn't dead, he was just badly wounded. He had been returning from the battlefield in the dark and a nervous sentry, thinking he was a Yankee goblin or something, shot him. After two years of hurry up, then wait, it wasn't a hardship to wait for news. We lost so many men at Chancellorsville that I guess they forgot about our regiment for a while, so we loafed in our tents. Once we packed up all the dead men's belongings, they finally remembered us. They even gave us some food, probably pilfered from the Yankees' endless supply of everything. Then the word flew around camp faster than wildfire. A new recruit named Billy Rawlins had shot Stonewall. They didn't rightly know what to do with him, so they sent him home.

After Stonewall died, the war went on and on and the Yankees kept us on the run. When it was finally over, those of us who survived went back to our homes. I was one of the lucky ones. Pa had kept the farm going somehow, despite the voracious armies trampling back and forth across poor, battered Virginia. I had only been home for a couple of months when I heard that the man who shot Stonewall Jackson, Billy Rawlins, had hanged himself. It seems his pa kept telling him that he killed the man who could have won the war for the Confederacy. I guess the damned fool kid must have believed him, because he went into the barn, threw a rope over a beam and ended his life . . . But that was a long time ago.

I hadn't thought about Billy Rawlins for many years. Seeing that soldier in Dahlgren's store reminded me about what had eaten so much of my soul away. It all came back to me from a distance, like hearing a voice on that new telephone invention: the useless waste of young men, the suffering that devastated so many lives, the ease with which we forgot the dead. All I could think of was that if I knew then what I knew now, I could have gone to see Billy. I could have told him that what he did was just one more crazy mistake in a succession of terrible events. That Stonewall couldn't have won the war. Hell, it was lost way before that. Only fools believed that we could win after the first year or so. The Yankees had everything. We only had pride and courage. Once they wore out our pride, courage just wasn't enough. But my understanding of things came much too late to help poor Billy. I couldn't help that trooper who lost his soul in the jungle. And I sure couldn't help any of the other innocents who don't start wars, only rush to fight them.

MY DAUGHTER, THE TYRANT

In 1968 my daughter was born and I needed to provide nourishment, suitable garments, and other appropriate offerings for this endearing bundle of protoplasm. This immediately changed my struggling poet's lifestyle. I went to work in an art gallery selling American art from the period 1900 to 1940, mostly to culturally devoid physicians and insensitive attorneys with social ambitions. The attorneys I understood. They were by nature and training manipulative and exploitive. After all, how else could you defend both sides of an issue with equal fervor, if you weren't a sophist? But the doctors? Those masters of life and death over their patients kowtowed to the gallery owner, a yahoo from the Bronx, who used to vend hot dogs at Yankee Stadium, until his uncle died and left him a prominent gallery. Well, I'm digressing a bit, but this is how I spent six days a week, Tuesday thru Sunday, ten to six, peddling culture.

We lived in Manhattan, in a tiny one-bedroom apartment on East 27th Street, near Lexington Avenue, that even with minimal furniture still imposed navigation hazards when voyaging from bedroom to bathroom. The only virtue of the apartment, besides the neighborhood, was a working fireplace. It was an unusual feature in a five story, post-World War II building, ultimately doomed to decay unless significantly renovated. The building cowered between large commercial loft buildings in Rose Hill, a semi-genteel neighborhood for upwardly mobile singles. Gentrification had not yet reared its intolerant head, so enclaves of Puerto Rican immigrants still thrived in tenements on Third Avenue in the Twenties, contrasted with new apartment buildings on the side streets. The shops and restaurants reflected the community. A few were pretentious, most were lower middle class, the rest catered to the poverty shopper.

Somewhere between the age of two and three, the innocent babe who bewitched me turned into an imp of Satan, with a disposition of sulfur and brimstone, and a will of tungsten steel. Somehow, Arla had been transformed into a creature of demand, who recognized no sovereign boundaries. It started with a request for a cat. I came home from work one day, drained from touting the virtues of the Ash Can School, the Precisionists and the Regionalists. I was greeted at the door by the welcoming committee. "Daddy. I want a cat." Of course I responded instantly like a loving, sensitive, doting father. "Absolutely not." I headed to my easy chair, content with my exercise of authority, until a tug on my arm brought me back to reality. "Daddy. I want a cat."

For the next three weeks, the cat blitzkrieg rolled each morning and night, before and after work, and all day Monday, my only day off. "Daddy. I want a cat." I resisted valiantly, until my wife crumbled. "Hon. A cat isn't much trouble and she really wants it." Defeat was inevitable, so I surrendered graciously and took Arla to the Bideaway Animal Shelter, with zero idea how to pick a cat. We walked past hundreds of cages, with hundreds of imprisoned felon cats, each desperate for release. Arla inspected each cage carefully, then moved on. After looking at an endless array of cats, big and small, and all colors of the spectrum, Arla stopped at one cage. The cat bounded to the door, meowed stridently, and Arla announced, "That's my cat, Daddy." I didn't know then that the orange colored calico had the nastiest disposition of housecats, which she quickly demonstrated as soon as she got to her new home. She also never meowed again.

After several weeks of Arla being clawed during her efforts to dress the reluctant cat in doll clothes, we had Wally the Walrus declawed. She got her name because of the way she scuttled along the rug, wiping her backside, after using the litter box. My suggestion that we return Wally was not favorably received. Wally and I waged a low intensity conflict, with the cat ambushing me and attempting to bite me, and my responding with a good, swift kick whenever she sprang at me. When she drew blood two mornings in a row, I proposed detoothing her, which Arla promptly vetoed. "Now, Daddy," she said accusingly, "you already took her claws. That's enough." So the cat and I settled into a tense state of détente, but I will admit that my response time to attack improved considerably. I was also more alert to my surroundings, both at home and outside, an inadvertent benefit that I never acknowledged.

Several months later, some friends invited us to visit them in Florida and we went on a vacation. They knew we had very little money, so except for air fare, they paid for everything, including a rental car. We made day trips all over southern Florida and Arla really enjoyed the seedy roadside tourist attractions, particularly the Parrot Jungle. We were on a back road, somewhere between Miami and Fort Meyers, real swamp-critter country, when we saw the most decrepit tourist trap yet: Alligator World. "Let's look at alligators, Daddy," Arla requested. My feeble attempt at avoidance, "They're probably all stuffed," was rejected. Alligator World actually had a very large alligator, probably still alive, but the surprise attraction was several large tanks, each with different sizes of hundreds of alligators, from babies to juveniles, crawling, swimming, wrestling, eating, or sleeping, that completely fascinated Arla.

Arla stared at the alligators, enrapt. After twenty minutes, I said, "It's time to go." "I want an alligator, Daddy." Finally. Something I could say no to. "That's not possible, sweetie." "Why not?" she demanded. I thought quickly. "They're not house pets." "Why not?" "Where would we keep one?" "In a small tank, Daddy." "What happens when he gets big?" "We'll give him to the zoo." I was rapidly running out of excuses, so I resorted to the tried and true. "We can't afford one." Faster than a slinking predator, a genuine red-neckus Americanus appeared out of nowhere. "'Taint much to get 'em." "How much?" I stalled. "Twenny dolla." I had to admit 'twerent much, so in desperation I tried the final excuse: "We couldn't take one with us. We're on vacation." "We can send ya un, mister," red-neckus volunteered. Trapped, I gave the man twenty dollars and wrote my address as illegibly as possible. As we left, I concealed my satisfaction that not even the FBI could decipher my address.

Arla never said another word about the alligator, and soon after we returned to New York City I forgot about it. Then several weeks later, a small box from Florida arrived. It was two inches by twelve inches by two inches, and crammed inside was a live alligator that had somehow survived the handling of the U.S. Postal Service in its long trip in a casket-like box. "Mister Totus," Arla said in greeting, as she picked him up. Mister Totus promptly bit her, she smacked him on the snout and off they went to play. The next day I went to the library on Third Avenue and 31st Street to learn the requisite alligator lore for Mister Totus's survival. Of course I was already plotting his accidental escape, when he would end up in a sewer, no doubt adding to a New York legend. I spoke to the same librarian from my previous visit, who had pitied my ignorance about cats, but recommended a book. This time she drew back from me, suspecting mental or moral unbalance. "We have no books on the care of pet alligators. There's a pet shop on 28th Street that sells reptiles. Perhaps they can help you."

Mister Totus got a tank and began his diet of tiny live worms that he chased, caught, and devoured. He took baths with Arla and she trained him not to bite her. How little Sheena managed that I'll never know. We had a short period of tranquility, until I came home from work one day and Arla showed me a second box from Florida. I knew instantly what it was, but not why. I had paid for one alligator that I hoped to never get. Now there was another one. Arla had courteously waited for me to come home before opening the box, so the sewer solution was out of the question. "Look, Daddy. It's Mrs. Totus." And Arla took her to Mr. Totus, who willingly shared his worms. A match hallowed by the postal service. Then another box arrived and this time it contained baby Totus, who was cold-bloodedly welcomed to the family.

The Totuses frequently appeared in Arla's best doll clothes, sparing the recalcitrant cat some indignities. Warfare between Wally and the alligator army took place when the alligators escaped from their tank, an occurrence that happened suspiciously often. Without claws, Wally could only try to grab the armored reptiles in her mouth and bite. The gators wriggled, twisted, squirmed, kicked, and bit back. Their teeth were sharp enough and their hides thick enough that Wally soon cried quarter. Truce reigned on the battlefield and the victors marched up and down the house at will, displaying a penchant for hulking as close to the fireplace as possible, whenever we lit a fire. Each day I waited for the next box to arrive from Florida, imagining that each one would be bigger and bigger. Fortunately, after a while we seemed to have received our quota.

Once again calm briefly prevailed in our domicile, except one morning when Mr. Totus somehow climbed into my bed and nipped me on the toe. Dire threats of handbag or shoe manufacturing convinced Arla that the bed was off limits to alligators. I should have known it was a false peace. I came home from work and was greeted with: "Daddy. I want a gerbil." I had grown up with dogs, bugs, frogs, and other creatures, but had no idea what she was talking about. "What the devil is a gerbil?" "It's this tiny, adorable, little furry animal." "How big?" "It fits in your hand." I went to the dictionary and looked it up. "It's a rat," I said. "No, Daddy. It's like a miniature bunny." I stared at her in amazement. "It's a rat." "No. It's not. Beth from pre-school has a bunch of them and she said she'd give me two boys for free, with a cage, and they only eat a little bit of lettuce each day."

Snoopy and Sam the gerbils joined our household the next day. They really were small and proved amusing when they ran madly 'round and 'round on their treadmill. By the third day they seemed to do most of their running at night, while I was trying to sleep. Despite vast infusions of oil and other lubricants, the treadmill kept squeaking. A week went by and I came home from work one evening to the next surprise. "Daddy. Look. Sam isn't a boy. He's a girl." He certainly was. There were eight teensy fluffballs snuggled against Sam. Well, they didn't take up much room and Arla couldn't have planned it, could she? So our family grew a bit more, and they didn't eat much lettuce. But a week later they were as big as Mama Sam, and running and flopping all over each other, day and night, in a cage designed for two or three at most. "Daddy. We need a bigger cage."

We got a bigger cage and divided Mama Sam's clan into two groups, one with Sam, the other with Snoopy. Wally redoubled her efforts to get into the cages, so I made sure the cages were out of her reach. Coincidentally, Wally was getting fatter daily, so its vertical attainments were becoming more limited. It didn't take long until the Sam clan multiplied and suddenly we had thirty-five gerbils. Was it the lettuce? The water? Only plaque multiplied faster. Arla named each one of them and would recite their lineage on a moment's notice. I built a larger cage and communal life thrived in gerbildom. Then I came home from work one day and Arla greeted me in tears. "Daddy. Snoopy's dead. I stepped on him and he's dead." After I offered sufficient sympathy, we proceeded with Snoopy's funeral. We put him in a tiny box, I said suitable words, then hummed some Chopin and we committed Snoopy's mortal remains to the incinerator.

Thus a new cycle began at chez animal domicile. The gerbils continued to prosper and multiply, so I built a long cage, with a hab-a-trail that got almost as much use as the Chisolm Trail. And with increasing regularity, I presided over gerbil funerals several times a week. The ritual was now solidly established. Arla would greet me at the door in tears with the mortality announcement and recite the lineage of the deceased. Consolation would take place, then words, then humming, then the final consignment to the incinerator. There were too many deaths to provide coffins for each formal occasion, but they all required the utmost solemnity. If I dared utter a sardonic remark, such as desiring a discount rate for my services, or other dissident comments, Arla's wrath was wondrous to behold. She turned a medusa gaze on me that instantly quelled rebellion.

The sedate order of things was disrupted when baby Totus became ill. Arla didn't notice at first that he stopped eating. Even her ground-air surveillance sometimes missed something. Then he developed some kind of infection that discolored his snout. We consulted the meager alligator book, the pet shop, the library, and finally the reptile keeper at the Bronx Zoo. No one had any answers. We tried salves, unguents, solvents, attars, oils, vitamins, minerals to no avail. Despite our best efforts, Baby Totus breathed his last. The poor gator never even got the chance to bite anyone. Baby Totus's funeral was grander than Snoopy's, if not quite as heartfelt. His box was more elegant, my words more sonorous, our humming more doleful, but at the end, he took the same journey to the incinerator, as had so many members of our household. I had a disturbing image of traveling the same route.

Mama Sam's offspring continued to spawn, maintaining a birth rate that far exceeded the mortality rate. The latest census estimated our gerbil population at somewhere between a hundred and fifty and a hundred and sixty rodents. Funerals took place several times a week, with the usual lamentations and ritual. One notable event was the day of the great escape. Somehow the large cage was knocked off its stand and dozens of gerbils made their break for freedom. Wally and Mr. and Mrs. Totus immediately began the hunt, complicating Arla's rescue attempts. When I came home, Arla shared her horror at discovering a gerbil tail sticking out of Wally's mouth. "It was disgusting, Daddy. I didn't know what it was at first, then Wally smiled at me and I knew. Ooky." I was exceptionally sympathetic during that particular funeral. As far as we could tell, most of the other escapees were recaptured alive.

It became necessary to add another large cage, since the old one was teeming day and night like a Bangladeshi hive in our tiny apartment. Mama Sam finally died, probably of exhaustion, yet the population continued to soar. Arla offered surprisingly little resistance when I insisted that we divest ourselves of some of our abundant gerbils and share them with the less fortunate. We started with the local pet shop, that actually bought twenty, for two dollars each. "See, Daddy. We'll make a lot of money." I tried in vain to explain that I had no ambition to be a gerbil tycoon, and pointed out that the randy rodents kept replacing their departed kin too rapidly. My next plan was to give a pair of gerbils to each of Arla's preschool classmates. A dastardly deed, I admit, but conceived only out of desperation. But no matter how many gerbils we got rid of, they reproduced faster and faster, until I yearned for a visitation of plague.

Arla had been remarkably relaxed during the gerbil crisis. Then I learned the reason. I came home from work and was greeted with: "Daddy. I want a dog." "Absolutely not," I refused imperiously. I had dogs most of my life and knew the work they required. "Daddy. I want a dog." "No way," I insisted, and the summer offensive was underway. But I knew the consequences of defeat and manned the trenches valiantly and vowed: "They shall not pass." And day and night Arla carried out her campaign with the relentless surge of a Tartar horde. I endured tears, sulks, snits, sobs, yells, screams, and hissy fits, but I didn't waver. I repelled every assault without losing my temper. I actually began to believe that there was light at the end of the tunnel. Foolish father.

I was relaxing at home on my day off and Arla was playing in the hall with her friend from ballet class. The apartment door was ajar so I could monitor the girls. Suddenly there was a horrible shriek. I raced to the door, threw it open, urgent to save my daughter from the clutches of a fiend and there she was, arms folded on her chest, gaze implacable, looking up at me with infinite determination. "Daddy, I want a dog." Sensing the imminence of defeat, I temporized. "I'll think about it." Arla smelled the nectar of victory. "For how long, Daddy?" "A couple of days," I replied weakly. "Two days, Daddy?" "Two days," I agreed. There really wasn't much to think about. I needed a deus ex machina to rescue me, but I didn't expect miraculous salvation. It was up to me to find a way out of my dilemma.

Two days later I was summoned to the Yalta Conference, where I was persuaded to concede Eastern Europe. "I don't know the first thing about getting a dog," I said, trying to play dumb. "When I was a kid they just came to me." "Look in the newspaper, Daddy." There was a community newspaper left on a table in the miniscule lobby and I went and got it. I found a notice for puppies and phoned. A mellifluous voice answered: "This is Cleopatra. I have your puppy." "But we haven't discussed it yet," I protested. "Don't worry. I'll be there in ten minutes." And she hung up. It took a minute or so for the shock to wear off, then I realized that I hadn't given Cleopatra my name and address. I called her back, but there was no answer. "I'll try her again later," I explained. Arla was remarkably composed. "All right, Daddy."

Ten minutes later the doorbell rang, I opened it, and there was a jolly-faced, enormously fat woman, with a bundle of fur in her arms. "I'm Cleopatra. Here's your puppy." "It's my dog, Daddy," Arla said, and took the newest invader from Cleopatra. All I could see were huge brown eyes and gigantic paws. "Those paws are awfully large," I ventured. Cleopatra patted me reassuringly. "All puppies have large paws." "Don't you know anything, Daddy?" Arla added scornfully. I had to admit that it sounded familiar and in desperation, as my defenses were crumbling about me, I said, "I don't think we can afford a dog. How much is it?" "It's all right," Cleopatra said soothingly. "You only have to pay for his shots.

Twenty-five dollars." Vanquished, I paid her, and off she sailed, a massive galleon bound for another shore, leaving Arla with her dog. I had no idea how Cleopatra found us without the address. Could Arla have engineered this transaction? No way. Only a defeated daddy could be that suspicious.

Arla played with her new acquisition for a while. Whenever she let it go, the puppy kept sprawling in different directions every time it tried to walk. Wally whomped him a few times, until Arla whomped Wally and instructed her not to molest the puppy. The puppy used the newspaper I spread for his personal business, without requiring any training. Another peculiar occurrence. Then we made a bed for the puppy in front of the fireplace with an old blanket, and he settled in for the night like the rest of the menagerie. Sometime later a strange noise woke me. I went into the living room, intent on protecting home and hearth, and discovered the source of the noise. The puppy was growing. I could actually hear him growing. For the next several weeks he kept growing longer and longer, without growing taller, until he made a dachshund look compressed. The few times we took him outdoors he was an object of public derision.

Our newest resident received a name, Beauregard T. Rassmussas, Beau for short. He responded to an identity by growing taller. Except for the enormous paws, he actually began to resemble a dog. To celebrate the canine emergence, we took him to Madison Square Park to the after-work dog gathering, to present him to doggie society. His debut was inauspicious. The male dogs attacked him, biting him, or knocking him down, despite his squeals for mercy. The owners were as malicious as their dogs, enjoying the helpless pup's torment. This was my first exposure to dog owners in many years and I was astonished at their cruelty and pathetic need to identify with their dogs. They treated them like overindulgent children, which suggested that they didn't have much of a life of their own.

Beau grew faster and faster and suddenly we discovered we had a Great Dane. The dogs at the park still attacked him, so we walked him in a separate area. He made friends with an older dog who took him under his wing and taught him how to run and fight. At seven months, Beau was quite large and had become formidable enough to intimidate most of the dogs who used to attack him. The owners were indignant that Beau had learned to defend himself, and objected strenuously when he wouldn't be bullied any longer. I was formally requested not to bring him to the dog run, because he was too belligerent. I could understand the vicious owners. I never understood how adult dogs could attack a helpless puppy. One more mystery in this inexplicable life.

We eventually got rid of all the gerbils. Mrs. Totus died when someone stepped on her during a party. Mr. Totus grew too big for us to keep and he went to the Bronx Zoo, where hopefully he led a long, happy reptile life. With only a cat and dog, we seemed like a normal family, but I knew it was an illusion. Arla turned her energies to the wider world of school and ballet class, but retained her strength of character. Arla was exceptional in that she never demanded things that cost money. She was generous, loyal, and honest, a person I admired. In my youth I had to struggle mightily to keep a pet, since my mother hated all things living. I never admitted that I took pleasure in Arla's efforts to acquire animal life, and I never felt bad when she attained her goals. It was a great luxury for me to indulge her at a time when I couldn't afford material things.

PURSUIT

"There he is. Let's get 'im," cried an impatient voice, as I hesitantly opened the main door. The other boys, more experienced in the chase, had waited to see which exit I would risk today.

I had left my sixth-grade class as soon as the three o'clock bell rang, but, as on almost every other day in the past few weeks, they were already waiting for me when I got downstairs. I muttered to myself, "If it wasn't for that lousy Mrs. Borgman stopping me from running, I would have gotten out before any of them." I dashed for the side exit that would force me to take the long way home. What made it even worse, was that many of the boys lived that way and could chase me further than if I went by Albany Avenue.

I slunk out the door, trying to conceal myself in a crowd of laughing, unpersecuted kids and warily looked around. I cautiously started down Farragut Road. I was just beginning to think I escaped for a change, when Joanie Collins waved to Artie, getting his attention and pointing to me. Artie was the biggest and oldest boy in the class. He was also the most favored by Joanie in the fumblings in the cloakroom when the teacher was late. I started running, cursing Joanie, finally accepting that she'd never go into the cloakroom with me. I still couldn't help wondering why they picked on me.

My vicious classmates ran after me, a mindless pack pursuing its prey. Artie was leading and the almost moronic Bobby Bryan was close behind. I saw Artie's long legs churning, as he slowly drew closer. I heard him holler in his deep voice, that always ended in an evil laugh: "Where ya going, Billy? Don't ya want to talk to yer old friend Artie?" "Why dontcha leave me alone?" I called over my shoulder.

I saw the railroad embankment ahead and decided to risk slowing down for the railroad crossing, instead of running further and using the underpass. I vaulted the low concrete wall and started up the weed-infested slope. All I had to do was cross the rock-filled tracks and they'd stop chasing me. I just reached the first track, when short, fat Milton Glasner, who was only brave when he was with the others, picked up a rock and threw it at me. The pack was disappointed that he missed. "See ya tomorrow, Billy," Artie called in a taunting voice. But I had escaped again, and there was always hope that plague or lightning might strike my persecutors. In the meantime, I could relax until tomorrow.

INTRUSION

Corinne Jones's legs ached as she trudged through the cold evening rain to the bus stop on Third Avenue. The poorly designed bus shelter only partially shielded her from the slanting downpour. She waited like a weary farm animal whose labor was done, yet the barn was still far away, for the bus that would take her uptown and across 125th Street to Harlem. She held the bag of leftovers under her porous old blue cloth coat in an effort to keep them dry for her granddaughter, Sharina. The thought of that beautiful child helped her endure the life eroding fatigue that was washing over her as relentlessly as the rain.

After a twenty-minute wait that seemed forever the bus finally arrived. Corinne hauled herself up the steps, swiped her fare card through the slot, and looked for a seat. She started up the aisle and saw Betty Ann, an older black woman who worked as a maid for the Swintons, a wealthy white family who were friends of her employers. Shortly after she went to work for the Pardees she met Betty Ann when they shared duties at an open house party. Betty Ann hated her employers in particular and whites in general. She tried to infect Corinne with her prejudice and started to tell her how to steal from her employers. Corinne stopped her abruptly and refused to have anything to do with her after that. Over the years Betty Ann had forgotten what caused her enmity, but she loathed Corinne and insulted her whenever they met. They often took the same bus home at night and Betty Ann would greet her each time: "You old bitch. Fuck you." And Corinne would respond: "You mean old hag." The ritual concluded, they would ignore each other the rest of the way.

Corinne said a silent prayer of thanks that she got a seat, because she didn't know if she had the strength to stand all the way to her stop at St. Nicholas Avenue. She took the bag of leftovers from under her coat, made sure it wasn't wet, then stared out the window into the glistening city night without seeing anything. She remembered when she first started working for the Pardees as a maid and Mrs. Pardee would inspect the leftovers bag to insure that Corinne wasn't taking unauthorized cuts of meat. The degrading search after the humiliation of being given leftover charity still pained her. She shook her head to clear it of the unwelcome thoughts and focused on Sharina.

Corinne had been taking care of her granddaughter since she was seven, when her father was killed in a drive-by shooting. The unfairness of her son's death was still an ache in her heart. Leshaun had been a good boy, then a good man, raising his daughter after his wife died of cancer. He was on his way home from work, just passing the corner where the drug dealers distributed the poison that was destroying so many of her people, when a car pulled up and gangbangers began firing. According to the policeman who told Sharina about her father's death when she was the only one he found at home, he died instantly. The police assumed that Leshaun was there for a drug buy and remained skeptical of Corinne's claim of his innocence, no matter how much she insisted that her son didn't use drugs. The awful memories were beginning to overwhelm her and she said a silent prayer that sent them away.

She sat there stolidly for a few minutes, as the bus rolled past the luxurious shops and restaurants that mocked the economically challenged who couldn't afford the prices of the new economy, or the old for that matter. She had willed herself long ago not to want things that she could never have and that way she was never tempted to steal. She didn't know if this made her a good person, but it made her an honest one. She had also learned to accept the unacceptable for the sake of her beloved granddaughter. The bus passed 96th Street and the shabbier stores and buildings sagged drearily in the corrosive rain. Corinne brooded about the last-minute instructions she received from her employer just as she was leaving. Mrs. Pardee told her in that false friendly tone of equality that she always used with Corinne: "The family will be going to Westhampton tomorrow morning, so you'll have to be here early. We'll come back Sunday evening, and we'll drop you at 125th Street where you catch your bus."

Corinne had assumed since it had been cold in early October that they wouldn't be going to the house in Westhampton again until spring. The Yankee weatherman betrayed her with a treacherous forecast of temperature in the seventies. She hated going to Westhampton. She had to sit in the front seat with the chauffer, Reggie, who listened to "gangsta rap" on his headset and never talked to her. Her only day off was Sunday, so now that was lost. To make it worse she couldn't bring Sharina, because she had a karate tournament on Saturday. The endless demands of the weekend sent a shudder of dread through her. The Pardees didn't bring the cook on weekends, so Corinne had to help in the kitchen and clean up afterwards. Between the Pardees and their guests they soiled more dishes, cups, glasses, and silverware than an army battalion just off field rations. And Reggie, who did the lawns and pool, would never dream of helping. Her only consolation was that Sharina would start college next September with a full scholarship. Once she was away at school, maybe Corinne could think about another job.

The bus started up the long hill to Harlem. Sometimes she wished that the hill was much higher, so they could look down on the rich folks below. Maybe then if there were race riots the hooligans could roll things down on the rich and not just destroy the poverty community. She shook her head and sent the bad thoughts away and pictured her granddaughter. Sharina was the light of her life, a wonderful girl who bubbled with joy, who was bright, talented, and an honor student bound for Harvard and a better future. The bus turned on 125th Street, stopped, and some noisy black youths wearing red bandanas on their heads swaggered on, shaking raindrops on the other passengers, daring them to object. Corinne looked straight ahead when they tried to meet people's eyes and they went to the back of the bus, boom box blasting curses and anger.

Corinne knew about gang colors. Her daughter Tabitha had run with a gang. Corinne had tried to stop her, but couldn't overcome the violent gang allure that eclipsed her dull, demanding days of school. In a desperate effort to stave off the inevitable, Corinne sent her to stay with relatives in North Carolina. Run-ins with the law and confrontations with the neighbors brought her back to Harlem, where she was beyond control. Her boyfriend turned her onto drugs and when her habit became too expensive he put her on the street as a prostitute, to pay for the white powder of obliteration. Sometime between tricking and shooting up, AIDS arrived and Tabitha slowly rotted away, decayed within and without, giving the gift of death to anyone who entered her wasted body. Then one day she didn't come home and was never heard from again. Corinne never found out what happened to her. She said a silent prayer for her lost daughter, pushed the stop signal and went to the rear exit so she wouldn't have to see Betty Ann.

Just before she got off the bus, Corinne risked a glance at the gang boys sprawled in the back, echoing the rap lyrics, yelling and cursing. Their red cotton bandanas reminded her of the field hands picking cotton who her mama had told her about. They were called handkerchief heads because of the cloth they wore to protect them from the sun. She couldn't help thinking that these violent boys were just as much slaves as the darkies of the past they so despised, except their master wore a different suit of greed. One of the boys noticed her staring at them. "Watcha lookin' at, ole black lady?" She turned away and scuttled off the bus, afraid that they might come after her and hurt her. As the bus drove away, the boy raised his middle finger at her, but she ignored it and quickly walked home.

The climb up five flights of stairs was more tiring than usual, but as she got to her door the image of her granddaughter raised her flagging spirits. Sharina was there, safe, sitting at the kitchen table doing her homework. Corinne's usual fear for the girl's well-being evaporated temporarily. "Hi, Gramma. You look tired." The kiss and loving hug rekindled her energy. "I'm all right. Mrs. Pardee told me we're goin' to Westhampton in the mornin' an' it just wore me down a bit." "Why can't that woman hire someone out there for the weekend? She couldn't care less about your welfare." "There are worse employers than Mrs. Pardee. At least she pays me for the extra day now." "It's not fair, Gramma. You don't get any benefits and if you get sick they won't help. They're so selfish. Why are they always intruding in our lives?" "It don't do no good to fret about them. I brought your dinner. Why don't you eat and forget them." "I hate eating their leftovers." "I know. But it's good food. Next year you'll be away at college and this'll be over." "You'll still be working for them." "We'll see. Once you're taken care of I can do somethin' else." "Oh Gramma, you've done so much for me." "You're a treasure, chile. Now eat while I go lie down."

The warm glow of Sharina's appreciation revived her and instead of going to bed she turned on the television set. It was the one-month anniversary of the World Trade Center disaster. She said a silent prayer for all the people killed that terrible day. The news was mostly about the bombing attacks on Afghanistan. After a humorous commercial that didn't amuse her, the big story was the third case of anthrax in Florida. It had become a criminal investigation, since they discovered that the source was man made. All the talk of biological attack by terrorists was scaring her and she hoped that the government would capture or kill the terrorists before they killed more Americans. She understood that the people in those Arab countries were poor and oppressed, but they shouldn't be allowed to murder innocent people. Her neighbor's husband died in the attack on the World Trade Center on

September 11th. He worked in the kitchen of that famous restaurant that was so high up and he didn't come down. He never did anything to Osama bin Laden.

Sharina finished her homework and came in and sat with her. "What are you watching, Gramma?" "One of those blond-haired ladies on CNN is tellin' us that we don't have to worry about anthrax. Now she's really got me worried." "There's nothing much we can do tonight. Tomorrow I'll ask Dr. Fairstone about it and he'll tell me what we should do. Now let's talk about something else." Corinne nodded agreement. "I was just thinkin' about how I used to take you with me to Westhampton when you were a little girl." "I always hated going there," Sharina said. "Those Pardee kids were so stuck up that when their friends were visiting they'd just ignore me, or order me around like a servant. But when they didn't have anyone else to play with, they'd behave as if those other humiliating things never happened. Sometimes I wished they drowned."

She looked at Corinne as if expecting her to be shocked, but she just smiled sadly: "I know they didn't treat you right, but I couldn't leave you alone back here in Harlem. You were just too young. I didn't like it any more than you did. Those Pardee kids are as selfish and inconsiderate as their parents. But I had no choice." "I understood that even then, Gramma. And it wasn't always awful. Sometimes Wesley behaved all right when no one else was around. It was that Amelia who really got me mad. One day she decided to play "Gone with the Wind" and she wanted me to be Mammy. When I refused she complained to her momma who told me I was being uncooperative. I told her that it was racially degrading for me to play Mammy, but I'd play Scarlet O'Hara if Amelia insisted on playing." Corinne laughed. "I remember that. It was one of the few times when Mrs. Pardee was at a loss for words. How old were you then?" "I was eleven." "I was so proud of you when you said that."

Sharina smiled. "Thanks, Gramma. Things got worse when I was thirteen and my body started developing. Reggie was always watching me. Even Mister Pardee looked at me. And Wesley was always trying to touch me when we went swimming." "I saw that. I was so happy when Doctor Fairstone got you that assistant counselor's job at the girls camp the next summer." "Me, too. I wasn't going to let any of them near me and I know it would have cost you your job if there was an incident." "We would have managed, chile." "I know, Gramma, but it would have been a problem and I'm glad it worked out. When Dr. Fairstone hired me the next year as a part-time assistant after school, I started learning so much about medicine that I decided to be a doctor. I'm so grateful to him."

Sharina didn't want her grandmother to feel neglected because she praised the doctor and said lovingly, "You're the best gramma in the whole world. Someday when I'm a successful doctor, I'm going to take care of you. I'll buy you a beautiful house, and nice furniture, and nice clothes . . ." "I don't need those things, chile. I have you and the lord." "But you've helped me with everything. You got me the job with Dr. Fairstone and the job at Wendell's Funeral Parlor." "I'm still sorry I did that. I don't know how you can work at that nasty place. The thought of you handlin' all those dead bodies makes my skin crawl." "It's safe, Gramma, and what I learn there will help me in medical school. Now let's talk about something else. I want to do something wonderful for you." "Well there is one thing." "What?" "When I die, I want to be buried someplace special." "Oh, Gramma, you're going to live a long time yet." "That may be, but that's what I want." "Then that's what you'll get." "You're an angel. Now give me a kiss and let's go to bed. It's gettin' late."

Sharina didn't think of their conversation again and her senior year of high school sped by in a welter of activities. Between school, her two part-time jobs, karate practice, and her new boyfriend,

Sharina was too busy to spend much time with her grandmother. Soon graduation day arrived and former president Bill Clinton, in a gesture to his Harlem neighbors, was the guest of honor and handed out diplomas. Corinne almost burst with pride when Sharina delivered the valedictory and President Clinton shook her hand. Then Sharina was off to Harvard for the early access pre-med studies program that would put superior students on a fast track. Sharina's scholarship covered dorm, board, books, fees, and tuition, so Corinne didn't have to worry about how she'd manage away from home. For the first time since the death of her son, the burden of responsibility for her precious granddaughter was gone. She could even start to think about what to do with her life.

Sharina wrote often for the first month or two, but when the first semester started her workload was enormous and she added to it with a part-time job in the anatomy lab maintaining the cadavers. She thrived on the challenges and loved the sheltered enclave of the university. She wrote Corinne that she had enough money to come home for Thanksgiving. She took the train from Boston on November 21st, avoiding flying like many Americans. She got home about nine p.m., unlocked the door and found her beloved gramma lying on the floor. She screamed, "Gramma," and rushed to her, but she was dead. Corinne's body was cold and stiff, so Sharina knew she had been dead for a while. She gently placed the lifeless head in her lap and cried silent tears that burned her cheeks.

As soon as she was able to stop crying, she phoned Dr. Fairstone and told him the sad news. He said he'd be there right away and the sound of his kindly voice set her crying again. He got there in five minutes and quickly examined Corinne. "She's been dead for about ten to twelve hours." "My poor gramma. If only I was here for her. I might have gotten her to the hospital in time." Dr. Fairstone shook his head. "It wouldn't have helped. She had a massive coronary that killed her instantly." "Did she suffer?" "No, dear. She didn't feel a thing." "Are you sure?" "Yes." He covered

Corinne with a blanket and turned to Sharina: "What kind of arrangements do you want to make?" "I don't know. I don't have any money." He patted her arm reassuringly. "I'll have Mr. Wendell take her to his funeral parlor and we'll work the details out later."

Mr. Wendell agreed to pick up the body at nine a.m. Dr. Fairstone made sure that Sharina was all right and offered her a sedative. "I don't need anything, thanks." "Then I'll see you in the morning. Call me if you need me." Sharina sat there quietly for a while, then walked through the apartment, idly touching some of her grandmother's things. She noticed the red light flashing on the answering machine and retrieved the first message.

"This is Mrs. Pardee, Corinne. I'm very disappointed that you didn't come to work. We have so many preparations for Thanksgiving that I really can't manage without you. Please call me." Sharina wanted to scream, but controlled herself and listened to the second message. "I don't know where you are, Corinne, but it's very irresponsible of you to leave me in the lurch like this. Call me at once." Sharina felt a blaze of hate rush through her and she dug her nails into her palms until her hands turned white.

It took Sharina a few minutes to bring herself under control, then she played the third message. "I realize you just don't care what happens to us. After all the years you worked for us, I expected a little more consideration." The rage she felt was ice cold as she reached for the phone and dialed the Pardees' number. When Mrs. Pardee answered in that detached, haughty voice that always suggested tennis whites, she said, "This is Sharina—" Before she could say anything else Mrs. Pardee interrupted: "Where is that grandmother of yours. Doesn't she know how important this holiday is?" Sharina took a deep breath. "My grandmother is dead, Mrs. Pardee." "I really don't appreciate your humor at a time like this." "Listen to me, you spoiled, self-centered—" "What did you call me? I told you she's dead. She died of a heart attack. Now do you have anything to say?" There was a brief silence, then Mrs.

Pardee said, "Well that's too bad. I guess I'll just have to call a temporary agency." Sharina slammed the phone down in disgust.

She didn't sleep at all that night. Every few hours she went into the living room and looked at the face of the only person in the world who loved her. Corinne looked older than she remembered, but more at peace, as if the stress of her responsibilities was over. Sharina whispered lovingly, "You were so good, Gramma. I'm so sorry that I didn't have the chance to do things for you." She cried for a while, then lay down to rest. Her thoughts kept coming back to the telephone messages from Mrs. Pardee and the infuriating phone call that followed. She knew what the Pardees were like, sheltered by wealth, insulated from the economic pressures that ordered the lives of the less privileged, and unaware of the needs of others. It wasn't that she expected them to be moved by the death of a black servant, which she now understood was only a mere inconvenience to them. It outraged her that Mrs. Pardee couldn't acknowledge that a person who worked for her for so many years had some significance. She decided that she'd give Mrs. Pardee another chance and call her in the morning, once Gramma was at the funeral parlor.

Mr. Wendell came for Corinne in the morning and invited Sharina to ride with him in the hearse. She declined and instead walked the few blocks. She felt remote from the people around her who were going about their business as if the best person in the whole world hadn't left her. She couldn't tell if the isolation she was feeling was from loss or numbness, but she seemed to be moving invisibly through the life around her. Dr. Fairstone and Mr. Wendell were waiting for her when she got to the funeral parlor. Mr. Wendell led her into the Heavenly Rest Chapel. "You just sit here and I'll bring your grandmother in." "You'll treat her nicely, won't you, Mr. Wendell?" "Yes, dear. She was my friend. Why don't you think about what you want done with her remains." She turned to Dr. Fairstone in despair. "I don't know what to do with Gramma."

"There, there," he said. "We'll put our heads together and figure out something."

She sat there in a daze without any sense of time passing until Mr. Wendell wheeled in a gurney. On it was one of his showroom coffins that contained her tiny gramma. She walked to the gleaming mahogany casket and looked down at the face that would never smile lovingly at her again. Tears gushed from her eyes and she silently vowed: *I don't know how, Gramma, but I'll find some way to make your burial special.* Dr. Fairstone waited patiently until she stopped crying. "We have to talk about the burial now. Did Corinne have any insurance?" "No, sir." "Does she have any family or friends who might help?" "I think we're the only ones." "What about her employer?" "You mean the Pardees?" "I didn't know their name." "Mrs. Pardee told me that it was very inconsiderate for Gramma to die at holiday time," Sharina said bitterly. "Perhaps they'll help with the funeral expense." "I don't think I can count on them for anything." "I'll contribute a coffin and the hearse to the cemetery," Mr. Wendell said, "but I can't cover the expense for the plot and headstone." "Thank you for your offer, but I don't have any money." "What if we cremate her? I'll do it for free." "I couldn't do that to her," Sharina said. "I'll call the Pardees again and ask for their help."

She phoned Mrs. Pardee, who sounded impatient at being bothered. "My gramma didn't have any insurance, Mrs. Pardee. I wonder if you can help me with the funeral expenses?" There was a long silence. "I don't think that will be possible." Sharina tried to contain her indignation. "She worked for you for a long time. Don't you feel any sense of obligation?" "We'll be happy to send flowers," Mrs. Pardee said coldly, "once you tell us where the service will be held. That's all we can do." "But I don't have the money to bury her properly," Sharina confided. "I'm sure you'll manage. There must be some place you can get help like the welfare bureau, or the NAACP." Sharina felt like strangling the ignorant, condescending woman. "You're some piece of work, Mrs. Pardee. My gramma slaved for you for years and that's all you can say? You can keep your stinking flowers." She hung up the phone without waiting for a reply and pounded the wall in frustration, while tears of rage poured from her eyes.

Dr. Fairstone and Mr. Wendell found her in the office sitting on the floor, slumped against the wall, crying. "I guess they wouldn't help you," Dr. Fairstone said gently. "We'll think of something, my dear. Why don't you wash your face and meet us in the chapel." Sharina went to the bathroom, rinsed with cold water, and pulled herself together. When she rejoined her friends they were discussing the funeral options. "Mr. Wendell has outlined the most practical arrangements," Dr. Fairstone said. "Cremation or burial at Potter's Field." "What's that?" "It's where indigents are buried in a cemetery on Staten Island," Mr. Wendell answered. Sharina was horrified. "I can't do that to my gramma." Dr. Fairstone tried to reason with her. "I understand that this isn't desirable, but there don't seem to be other choices." "I won't do that to her. I promised her something special. Let me think about it." "I have to get back to my patients. I'll come back when office hours are over." "Thanks, Dr. Fairstone. I really appreciate your help." "I wish I could stay with you, but my patients are worried about anthrax or other biological attacks. I'll see you later." "I'll walk you to the door," Mr. Wendell said.

Sharina sat in the chapel, brooding about her lack of choices and looking at the coffin that held her beloved gramma. She couldn't come up with any solutions to the problem. Every time she tried to concentrate, hateful images of the Pardees kept intruding. Mrs. Pardee's callous indifference was ripping through her with stabs of rage. A cold fury channeled her thoughts and helped focus her mind. She remembered a Pardee family funeral that she went to when she was a child. Her gramma was compelled to give up her Sunday and attend, and she took her along because there was no one to leave her with. She vaguely recollected a long ride to a Long

Island cemetery that seemed like an enchanted forest, with clumps of large old oak and maple trees that lined the walks. She had asked wonderingly, "Who lives in those big stone houses, Gramma?" She understood now that her gramma had carefully considered her answer: "Some people are put there by their families when they die." "Will we go there when we die?" "No, chile. Only the rich people go there." "Where will we go, Gramma?" "We don't have to worry about that for a long time."

The picture of her gramma's sweet, loving face when she said that brought more tears to Sharina's eyes, but her mind was crystal clear. Suddenly a wild idea flashed through her: *I'll put Gramma in the Pardee family mausoleum.* At first it sounded crazy, but the more she considered the idea, the more comforting it became. She basked in the wave of pleasure that rolled over her as she imagined Gramma resting in the splendid family tomb of the rich Pardees. After a few moments, more practical thoughts seeped in. How would she get Gramma to the cemetery? How would she get her into the mausoleum? Did she need a coffin? She had never been in a mausoleum, so it was a place of mystery. Did the bodies lie around in piles? On tables? In boxes? Frustration raced through her for her ignorance. She tried to control her swirling emotions and decided to ask Mr. Wendell about mausoleums, but not tell him about her far-fetched idea right away.

Mr. Wendell was on the phone when she walked into his office and he gestured to her to sit down. She fidgeted tensely as he wheedled someone at the medical examiner's office about the interpretation of his contract to inter John and Jane Doe bodies for the city. When business was slow he was eager for the extra income from indigent funerals. If business was good he didn't want to waste time on the low-fee jobs. His special efforts to befriend the clerks who assigned the jobs included cash, gifts, and other incentives. He began to trust Sharina after she had worked for him for a while and he kept few secrets of his day to day operations from her. He made exaggerated funny faces for her benefit as he talked and she managed a weak smile of appreciation for his efforts to ease her sorrow. He finally hung up the phone, and shook his head. "My mama would turn over in her grave if she heard me arguing all the time about dead bodies, hee-hee."

She looked at him intently, considering how to present her wild idea, but he made it easy. "Have you decided what to do about your grandmother yet?" he asked in his professional voice of comfort. "I've thought about it and I've come up with a plan that I want to tell you about, but please don't interrupt me till I'm done. Okay?" "Sure. Go ahead." "I considered the choices and couldn't accept them because I promised Gramma a special burial and at first I didn't know what to do because I didn't have any money and I got madder and madder at the Pardees for not caring about her and I remembered they had a big family mausoleum and I decided I want to put Gramma into their mausoleum without their knowing, and—" "What?" "You said you wouldn't interrupt." "Where'd you get this crazy notion?" "Can I finish?" "Yeah." "Well I need your help to do it." "Girl, you're outta your mind." "That's the only way I can think of to do something special for her."

He stared at her strangely, then burst into laughter. "In all my years in mortuary science that's the craziest thing I ever heard." "Why? Once she's in there no one will know. It's just a matter of putting her in there. You should know how to do that." "You want me to do it?" he asked in amazement. "Who else? You're her friend. I'll help you. Nobody else has to know." "Do you have any idea what you're asking?" "Yes. If I had another choice I'd do it." "What about Dr. Fairstone?" "I won't tell him. He's a wonderful man, but he's set in his ways and I don't think he'd approve." "Are you telling me I'm not ethical?" "No, Mr. Wendell. He's old and wouldn't understand. You're a smart businessman. You know how complicated everything is." "You're a cunning devil. You think some flattery will get me to do it?" "I'm asking you as her friend."

He got up and paced behind his desk. "Let me think about it." A wave of gratitude raced through her. She rushed to him and kissed him on the cheek. "Thanks, Mr. Wendell. I knew you'd help." "I didn't agree yet. Now be quiet and let me think."

He sat down at his desk and leaned his head on his hands. She waited quietly until he asked, "Are you sure this is what you want to do?" "Do you have a better idea?" "No." "Then this is what I want." "Let me tell you what's involved. We gotta get the death certificate from Dr. Fairstone and tell him you decided to cremate her. The next day we go to . . . what's the name of their cemetery?" "I don't know, but it's the Pardee family mausoleum." "That's all right. I can get the information on the Internet. Then we drive there in a private car, hope one of my batch of keys will open the mausoleum door, find a good shelf, put her in, then get out without anyone noticing us." "That doesn't sound too hard." He snorted. "Right. And what if we get caught?" "I'll take all the blame." He shook his head. "You're as hard headed as your grandma." Then he laughed loudly. "But I like the idea of double dipping. I'll do it."

Now that she had help and a plan, a feeling of euphoria took over and everything seemed dreamlike and remote, as if it were happening to someone else. When Dr. Fairstone came back that evening she told him that she had decided on cremation. He sat with her for a while and his presence was comforting. She hugged him when he said good night and thanked him for being a good friend. Mr. Wendell suggested that she go home and sleep for a while, but she said she was too revved to leave. She looked over his shoulder while he searched the net until he located the cemetery. He explained to her that they couldn't put Corinne in a coffin because they wouldn't be able to manage it by themselves and they might be noticed if he brought extra help. He went to put Corinne in a plastic body bag and Sharina said she could do everything else, but she couldn't put her gramma in the bag. Mr. Wendell left her in the office while he made the final preparations and she dozed off.

She woke up in the morning with that odd sense of detachment that sometimes occurs when waking up in a strange place. Mr. Wendell brought fresh coffee and a donut for her that she devoured voraciously. They left the funeral parlor for Gramma's last ride at ten a.m. The traffic was light and within a few minutes they were crossing the Tri-Borough Bridge. The day was warm and clear and the sun glistened on the dirty face of the East River, concealing the detritus and pollution bequeathed to the waterways of America. She looked without seeing as they rolled along the Long Island Expressway and barely noticed when they turned into the cemetery. It took a few moments until it registered that they had arrived. She looked around curiously and found that the fabulous burial ground of memory was just another cemetery.

Mr. Wendell consulted a map of the cemetery that he had downloaded from the net and drove straight to the Pardee mausoleum. No one paid any attention to them. He got out of the car, walked to the massive metal door with his large ring of keys, tried some, and in a few moments he swung the door open. He looked around carefully and made sure no one was watching them. He went to the car, motioned her to come help him, then opened the trunk and removed the body bag. They carried it into the mausoleum and put it down on the stone floor. Mr. Wendell checked the shelves and found one that contained Beatrice Pardee, 1882-1957. He opened the decorative marble panel, then the wooden door. They picked up the body bag and slid it behind Beatrice's coffin, where it couldn't be seen. "If you want to say anything, do it quickly," Mr. Wendell said urgently. "We need to get out of here without being discovered." She stood there silently and finally whispered, "Goodbye, Gramma. I love you."

Mr. Wendell closed the shelf door and quickly replaced the marble panel. He rushed her out the door, locked it, hurried them to the car, then drove out of the cemetery. Once they were on the highway, he yelled triumphantly, "Nobody saw us. Whatta ya think of that, kid?" "I don't believe how easy it was." "It's like anything else in the world. If you know what you're doing and go about it naturally, as if you belong, nobody notices." "I'll never forget this, Mr. Wendell. If there's every any way to repay you I will." "That's all right, girl. It was a rush doing that. You don't owe me anything." For the rest of the ride he babbled on, keyed up by his adventure, and didn't notice her silence. She sat there quietly, locked in memories of her beloved gramma. Just as they got to the glittering bridge that led back to Harlem, she thought: *I did it, Gramma. I made your burial special. Now you'll rest in that grand stone mansion for the dead with the Pardees and not have to clean up after them. I hope you won't mind being there. It's the best I could do.*

THE ENCOUNTER

Tim was just opening the door to speed the unwanted guest on his way, when Raimond turned abruptly.

"I would like you two to have dinner with me next week. Is Tuesday good?"

"Fine, Raimond," Tim answered. "That's very nice of you."

"It is nothing. I like you both very much. I will make for you a nice dinner."

"Thanks again, Raimond. We'll see you Tuesday."

"Goodnight, Tim. And you, adorable girl, may I kiss your hand? You do not mind, Tim?"

"No, no. Not at all," he replied, struggling to remain patient.

"Goodnight then, Marian."

"Goodnight, Raimond . . . What time shall we come?"

"Seven. Come at seven. Until then, au revoir."

"Goodnight," she said again.

Once Raimond finally left, Tim turned to her. "Jesus, Marian, I thought that creep would never close the door. My jaw hurts from all that smiling and polite crap."

"Tim! What if he came back for some reason and heard you? You know how thin the door is."

"Then I would get up, bow, say enchanté, monsieur, and look at him with a sardonically, quizzical expression."

"Oh, you're terrible. You make fun of everyone we meet."

"Well you gotta admit that this guy's a real character."

"I think he's cute."

"Cute! Bless my backside, cute. Now would you care to tell me how you managed to acquire this one?"

"Do you always have to be so sarcastic?"

"Well, when you come home with some old Frenchman, full of monkey glands, simpering over you like an absolute ass, do you expect me to treat him like Anatole France?"

"He's just a nice old man who helped me. There's no reason for you to get jealous and carry on this way."

"Jealous? Of that worn-out old Billy-goat? You really amuse me sometimes. Did you ever stop to think that I may be tired of being pleasant to all the strays you bring home? If just once you'd drag home someone with a trace of intelligence or sincerity, or even an honest, unpretentious jerk. But you always collect these complete idiots, from sixteen to sixty, who think that because you act friendly they're going to get laid."

"I don't know why you always pick on me. You'd think I was doing something wrong all the time," she sniffed.

"Maybe if you slept with all the weirdos you bring home for me to meet, you'd start to learn something about people. All these guys want to do is get into your pants. After they talk to you for a while that's what they think is going to happen. Shit. I can just hear what goes on in their heads: 'I don't know how it happened, but this girl really believes what I'm telling her. Her husband can't be too bright. It should be pretty easy to get him out of the way and get her on her back.'"

"Tim Brandon, you're horrible and vulgar."

"At least when I want to get into your pants, I don't say, 'Look at me, I'm so intelligent, so clever, so brilliant, let's fuck.'"

"Oh, Tim. You know that I don't believe everything they tell me."

"Well let's not go into that. You started to tell me how you met this one?"

"You're not going to make fun of me?"

"I'll be as solemn as a hippopotamus."

"Tim!"

"All right, all right. Tell me."

"Well I was carrying my new vacuum cleaner from the store and it was pretty heavy, but I wasn't having too much trouble until I got out of the subway. Then it started getting heavier, and I had a hard time getting to the bus. This man was standing at the bus stop and when he saw me struggling, he came to my assistance. He was very polite and insisted on getting off at my stop and helping me home. I asked him to come upstairs and have a drink, and he asked, 'Wouldn't your husband mind?' I said no, but he still didn't want to come upstairs. But I insisted, so he finally came."

"All right. It was very nice of him to help you, and it was very courteous of you to invite him up for a drink, but couldn't you see that he was boring me to death? I mean, he sat there babbling to us for three hours."

"Oh, Tim. Couldn't you see how lonely he was?"

"Lonely! I'm working five days a week and going to school five nights a week, and on the weekends, I have to study. Maybe I'm lonely and would like to spend a few hours with my wife, without these crazy characters that you always seem to attract."

"Timmy, are you feeling lonely? Do you want your little girl to pay attention to you? Is my big boy feeling neglected?"

"If you start that baby talk, I swear I'll punch you right in the eye."

"But, Timmy . . ."

"Oh, come here, you little loon."

"That's it, Timmy. Put your arms around me, instead of yelling at me."

"You always feel so soft . . ."

"I love when you hold me, Timmy . . ."

"I'm not one of your waifs, but I'd like to get into your pants. Do you think it can be arranged?"

"If you carry me to the bed."

"Done."

"I love you so much, Timmy."

"I love you, baby."
"Hurry, Timmy. Hurry."

VARNER'S DILEMMA

Henry Varner had reached the point where he had two complaints: he was born, and he didn't have the courage to kill himself. Every calamity paled after he accepted these facts. His subsiding into apathy from frustration with his unsatisfactory life was easily welcomed.

His parents were grey slabs of people from St. Louis, who performed their roles in complete obscurity. His father's drug store, harbor for his secret shame, yet birthplace to his visions, was the only demand on his time when he reached high school. Grammar school had passed in a mist with no commendations, no criticisms, no fights, and no fumbling in the cloakroom with budding maidens. But high school was different.

In Henry's sophomore year, his father installed a soda fountain in the drug store, and stationed Henry behind the soda fountain. Suddenly Henry was in the public eye. He wilted under the eyes of his classmates, when formerly he passed in a translucent haze. The immediate assaults of pleaders for credit, blossoming socialites who needed recognition, idle young ladies practicing both flirtations and sneers at his white cap and jacket nearly overwhelmed him, until he discovered the secret dream.

The seeds of the secret dream were planted at age twelve, when Henry began to live on the planet fantasy. He peopled a heroic world with imperious Tarzans, regal gunfighters, and dashing hussars, who practiced a fumbling sexuality of kisses and rubbing bodies with exquisite young beauties. At sixteen, firmly established behind the soda fountain, the planet fantasy had become more complex. Gone were the poetic imaginings of Africa, the wild west, and the courts and battlefields of Europe. In their place melodrama was born. Henry drew his cast from the young people who patronized him at the soda fountain. He used the boys he envied as enemies to always be defeated, and the girls he hopelessly coveted as beauties to be saved, then scorned, when they gratefully offered themselves.

Henry managed to build a shallow wall of superiority from his fantasies that enabled him to face his day to day life with a minimum of terror, since his foes were so easily vanquished. But growing sieges battered great chunks from his defensive wall, as his grey ineptness became more obvious in his fumblings with the high school damsels. So in his desperate search for a bulwark and some relief from the guilt of midnight masturbations, he discovered Miss Claymore.

Julia Claymore was the pride of a large clan of Missouri Claymores. All ignorant, uneducated farming people, they lavished their admiration for "eddecatin" on this prodigy who had actually studied for a year at the Art Institute, in Chicago. Rapidly realizing that she was just one of the vast horde of Midwestern artists who yearly assailed Chicago, she realistically evaluated herself as a star of lesser magnitude, then accepted the first decent teaching post that she was offered. She invaded the small St. Louis high school like Grandma Moses returning with her shield. By the end of her fifth year in the school she convinced herself that she had renounced a career of greatness to illuminate the path for promising youth.

Julia Claymore devoted herself to the discovery of talent. She actually knew little about art, but being decisive in her role as illuminator, she became as glib as a salesman. Any student who could draw a straight line was promised the ultimate fame of Da Vinci, Michelangelo, and Renoir (she had thick books about Da Vinci and Michelangelo, and there was rumored to be a Renoir somewhere in St. Louis), if they would only obey her directions.

Each term she managed to tempt one or two innocents into becoming famed artists, never giving up her dream to launch some genius and bask in reflected glory. She never discovered what happened to her protégés after they left the nest, because by the time their hopes were defeated, there was not even the shaft of venom left to hurl at that fool teacher who led them to disaster. So Julia Claymore worked on and waited for her pupils to find the light.

Henry had developed the habit of drawing costumes for the characters in his fantasies during Miss Claymore's art classes. He kept his sketches in a loose-leaf notebook that he always carried with him. One day he was summoned to his grade advisor's office during his art class and he left the notebook on his desk. Miss Claymore, peering at the work her students were doing, paused at Henry's desk and idly flipped open his notebook. On seeing a sketch of an elaborate evening gown she curiously turned a few pages, uncovering more attempts at costume design. She immediately decided that the hitherto unnoticed hunk of protoplasm, Henry Varner, a vague reference in her record book, would become an eminent fashion designer.

Henry returned to class, unaware of the revolution that had taken place in his life. He timidly said, "Yes, Miss Claymore," when he was requested to see her after class. The sudden sign of recognition made Henry apprehensive, since he had always avoided contact with his teachers.

After class, Miss Claymore, beaming at her newest discovery, asked Henry why he never showed her his attempts at design. Henry, thrown into complete panic and confusion, tried to deny this onslaught into his fantasies. But Miss Claymore insisted that his light must illuminate the world, so he helplessly placed himself in her hands. Miss Claymore's hands decided that Henry's future development would be a secret nurtured between them, until his glorious abilities captured the attention of the civilized world.

Henry went to work that afternoon at the soda fountain in a trance. During that day he forever closed the dream of melodrama and tasted the first fruits of creative ambition. The watchword of Henry's life became *When*. When I am famous . . . When I am recognized . . . When I am rich . . . When I am loved . . . New power came to Henry. He looked at the boys and girls who clustered around the fountain with disdain, vowing that they would all realize someday that they could have been his friends, if they had only been smart enough to recognize his genius.

Every spare moment in the daytime Henry was in the library, reading everything he could find about fashion design. He walked the streets with pad and pencil, maniacally sketching every helpless female he passed. Many stared in resentment at his rude interest. One woman complained to a policeman that a crazy young man was drawing dirty pictures of her. But even this degradation was survived by the passion of burning creativity. At night, after Henry's parents retired to their room, he filled notebook after notebook with styles looted from a thousand magazines, and from women that he saw in the street.

Henry's next two years in high school passed with a routine sameness: school, working at the soda fountain, sketching constantly, and secret confabulations with Miss Claymore, who dangled fame and fortune like a carrot before a donkey. So the time passed, and Henry worked and Miss Claymore schemed and gloated about Henry's glories to come.

One month before graduation, Miss Claymore realized that another disciple was about to leave her and enter the incommunicable world that had devoured all her previously launched pupils. She decided that she had suffered enough ingratitude and that just once her heroic efforts for her "bringers of the new renaissance" should be appreciated. After many hours of threatening, pleading, and offering tantalizing hints of recognition, Henry was convinced that he must allow her to sponsor a school showing of his designs.

Students were conscripted from the art class and under Miss Claymore's artistic direction, plastered the entire school with Henry's sketches. Parents, faculty, and students were cordially invited to attend the premier that would launch a great man's career. And here began the real tragedy of Henry Varner. Not one person who attended the exhibit had the faintest idea if Henry's work was good or bad. So for reasons such as the school had never had a true genius, no one wanted to appear ignorant before his peers, and certainly no one wanted to hurt Henry's feelings, Henry was hailed as the greatest innovation since brassieres.

Henry's salvation of retiring to the obscurity of the soda fountain and his melodramas was completely demolished by the wine of praise. He confronted his parents under the influence of fame's first embrace and declared that he was going to New York, to make himself available to the finest shops, destitute without his wondrous talents. His parents, utterly routed by this ferocious onslaught on their grey lives, suggested that he remain in the security of the drug store. When Henry's face changed from white to red to dangerous purple, they surrendered and gave him train fare to New York.

Many of Henry's classmates gathered at the railroad station to bid farewell to the brave genius who would conquer the world. While Henry was getting on the train, ticket in hand and cardboard valise in the other, Miss Claymore sat in her tiny office in the art department, rubbing her hands in delight at the swollen prestige her departing pupil had brought her.

Henry's trip to New York was uneventful. Although it was his first trip away from home, he was oblivious to the wonders of the unknown land that the train passed. All his waking moments were spent listening to the secret whispers of the wheels, promising fame, fame, fame . . . When the train arrived at Grand Central Station, in New York City, Henry, carried by his blind belief in destiny, didn't experience the fear and confusion that assailed most adventurers on reaching the fabled city. He passed through the station as if he arrived in New York every day, got into a taxi, and ordered the driver to take him to a cheap hotel. The cab passed towering buildings, dazzling theater marquees, and crowds of scurrying people, but Henry sat, swollen and pompous, ignoring the tantalizing glimpses of the city.

The driver took him to Broadway in the seventies and left him at a hotel fallen on decayed gentility. He drove off mumbling, when Henry, ending his first taxi ride, neglected to tip him. He entered the hotel, registered for seventy dollars a week, was led to a tiny cubicle that contained one green pock-marked iron bed, one green pock-marked iron dresser, one straight-backed wooden chair, one porcelain sink spattered with rust, and a tiny metal closet, painted the same bile green as the walls and ceiling.

The room, a suitable crypt for Edgar Allen Poe, was viewed with delight as Henry's first place of his own. His room at home had been three times larger, light and airy, but that was forgotten in his enchantment at being in the city. The valise was left unpacked on the bed, while he looked up the addresses of the foremost fashion houses and shops in the phone book. He knew that they were just waiting for his wondrous talents to appear. Then he went downstairs to a nearby restaurant.

Dinner passed in a mystic haze, as Henry devoured the poetry of the names and addresses of the fabled shops, so long a vision, now about to become a reality. He returned to the hotel, acknowledged the salute of the desk clerk with the aplomb of a jaded magnate, entered his room, quickly unpacked, and went to bed.

Henry awakened at eight a.m., soaped his hands, rinsed his face, squeezed two or three prominent blackheads, cleaned his teeth with hot water and his right index finger, combed his straight black hair, dressed in his good blue suit, then went out into the new world. By three p.m., having had his services rejected by a dozen shops, frequently with scorn and derision, he began to wonder if he was going about things properly. Henry walked uptown along Central Park West, completely immersed in a fantasy. His envious friends in

St. Louis had written to all the good designers in New York, warning them that he was coming. Fearing to be eclipsed, they decided not to give him the opportunity to show his ability.

He had dinner in the same restaurant as the night before, a small, steamy Chinese dungeon, crammed with shabby diners and hurrying waiters in grimy grey jackets, who were short, muscular, and looked like Tong hatchet men. With about the same knowledge of life in New York as life on Venus, Henry accepted everything he saw with complete equanimity, only disturbed by the day's rejections.

The next day, Henry tried the leading fashion houses with the same results, though perhaps he was treated with more contempt. But at the last stop, a sympathetic receptionist suggested that he try to get a position as a stock boy or shipping clerk, until he became experienced. Henry, still believing the myth of immediate fame, spun far from the battlefield in the security of a St. Louis high school, dismissed this advice without a moment's hesitation. He vowed that he would find some way to present his sketches to the leaders of the fashion industry, who were kept in ignorance of his existence by jealous competitors.

One week passed in a desperate, futile pilgrimage to every known fashion house and shop, without success. Henry had the first glimmers of realization that New York might not be immediately conquerable. His money was beginning to run out, so he decided to take a job as a stock boy, or anything else that he could find in the fashion industry. Another week passed without his finding a job, but he overheard a conversation about employment agencies, and decided to go to some. The first agency he tried found him a position as an assistant buyer trainee in a resident buying office, at a hundred and twenty-five dollars a week.

The first week of work was excruciating torment. Henry had grown up a victim of the myth of the sweetness of women, with the exception of a few pert girls, who would certainly mellow with time.

His new office was nothing like that. The women warriors of Hembel & Drang, Inc., occupant of three floors on West 36th Street, were born for conflict. Even more profane and aggressive than men, they had no hesitation in screaming, cursing, and abusing anyone who appeared on the horizon. He walked timid and fearful through the howling jungle of berserk women.

He reached the heights of terror and shame when the merchandising manager, Miss Gorter, an angelic looking old lady, who reminded him of his paternal grandmother, came charging out of her office like an insane fury, yelling, "Doris, you dirty bitch, where are you?" over and over, until Doris, one of her assistants, was discovered cowering in the ladies' bathroom. Henry returned to his hotel that evening in a comatose shock, stunned by the revelations of woman's character. Yet that night he managed to write an arrogant, boasting letter to his parents.

Dear Mom and Dad,

New York's sure a swell place. I've made all kinds of slick friends, who really like me, even a few girls. I've been looking around trying to decide where I want to work, but I haven't made up my mind yet. Everybody's really been swell to me, taking me to parties and all sorts of places where I've met a lot of famous people. How's everyone at home? Say hello to everyone for me, and tell them that I'm really making out fine. Please write to me.

Your son,

Henry

Then to bed and a night of dreamless sleep, bewildered awakening, weekend spent alone, walking, eating, staring at the forbidding face of the city.

Henry's life in the great city became a dreary routine; work, eat, sleep. He lost all interest in his sketches, lost forever the myth of fame and lost the fanatical determination to succeed. His job lasted exactly three weeks. On a Friday, that turned out to be his last day, they fired him. They told him that he just didn't have enough drive and he couldn't succeed as a buyer with such a mopey attitude. He left, paycheck in hand, wondering what to do next. He knew that after his proud departure he could not return to St. Louis, but no other options seemed clear.

Henry went home to the tawdry hotel and the desk clerk reminded him that the rent was overdue. He went up to his room feeling trapped and alone. He sat by the window that looked out on an airshaft opposite a room as seedy as his. Despair rolled over him like a languid wave, breaking on a crumbling shore. He couldn't go back, yet he didn't see how he could stay. Henry determined to decide his fate in the morning. As he drifted off to sleep, vague images of home floated through the mind. The last thing he remembered was reaching towards the soda fountain, to mix a drink, but he never got there.

EXTENDED MEETING

The benches in the New York City Clerk's office were hard and uncomfortable. The wood was worn and shiny from nervous and impatient squirmings. The room was dim and shabby, wearied from processions of the city poor, eager to pay the few dollars for the privilege of marriage, or not eager, but complying with demanding families, resenting the notices of *do*s and *don't*s, murmuring to the indifferent walls. And behind barred windows, clerks in funereal voices, never calling names fast enough to spare the nervous couples the glances of others. The eyes that have seen it all before; waiting, birth, death, the history of in-betweens, waiting.

(Visions stillborn or departed . . . Nightmare benches crumbling unseen, losing atoms to impatient squirmings. Weary room, deaf to processions of city people, spilling dollars across counters in front of clerks who have seen it all before: the testimony of birth, the swear of fitness. Waiting, birth moment until death. The history of in-betweens. Proclamations do and don't on fading walls. Faces eager or uneager. Failings of conversation. Waiting. Knells the indifferent voice, names. The marriage place, City Hall. Beginnings.)

Spring brought Allen and Rhoda to marriage. Spring, parents, unknowing, too much desire, but mostly spring. They first met in the Hunter College Library, in a building near Park Avenue. Allen was a night student and had left work early that day to do some last-minute studying for a chemistry exam. He didn't notice who he sat next to. Rhoda attended Hunter College in the Bronx, with its urban luxury of campus. She had made the subway voyage to 69th Street for a lecture, then stayed in the library to study for a chemistry exam the next day. She watched him fumble with text and notebook without finding a placemark. She sat losing concentration in the restless hush of libraries. When she heard Allen mumble a formula aloud and get stuck at the end, she provided the answer: "C16." He looked up in surprise. "What?" "C16. The end of the formula."

He stared blankly at her, until she said, "Check it in the book." The reference to the book brought recognition and they laughed for a moment, then offered the questions and complaints of college students. They parted later, without exchanging names.

Allen worked for an insurance company headquartered on 42nd Street as a junior accountant. His salary of two hundred and ninety dollars a week, with two raises in two years and another expected, barely enabled him to support himself. He lived alone in a furnished room, had no friends, and very few dates with girls. The death of his mother when he was nineteen had brought changes to his life that made a difference day to day. His father, suddenly freed from the distasteful burden of his ailing wife, stopped talking of his hope that his son would be an engineer, although Allen's lack of higher mathematics had already doomed that hope. Then his father started bringing home women from the shirt factory where he worked. His son soon became an encumbrance.

Allen had left home, found a room and job, switched from day to night school and made a plan to become an accountant. He solved most of his problems by plugging away at them. What he couldn't solve, he ignored, until one day he had a social problem. He was invited to a party by someone in his office, who only asked him out of politeness. He couldn't decide whether to go alone, or not at all. He took his problem to the local Greek diner for lunch. He waited on line for a place at the counter, looking out the window at people hurrying somewhere, and he saw the girl from the library walk by. With unaccustomed bravery, he sought the answer to his problem. He dashed out of the diner, followed her until she stopped to look in a shop window, walked quickly past her, then turned back to meet her accidentally.

Rhoda wasn't attractive. Her mother began to punish her for this crime when she was four years old. She became a make-believe child, pretending a secret life in her head. Her father always sat in the imitation green-leather armchair, reading his newspaper, only pausing to tell her to obey her mother. When she was twelve her breasts began to grow, despite her mother's strenuous objections. By the time she started high school, she was used to boys brushing their shoulders against her. When she was sixteen, she submitted to backseat copulations in her boyfriend's car. She felt nothing in the drive-in sex, though sometimes the clumsy pokings made her sore. But the attention was delicious, until she overheard him tell another boy that he did it to her for old glory, with a flag over her face.

Rhoda wasn't happy. After graduating from high school, she worked during the summer as a file clerk. The boys at work were the same as in high school. Older, but the same. She went to college dreaming of romance. Not someone on the football or basketball team, but perhaps the fencing team. She joined a sorority, but they were nicknamed the Fuzzie-Wuzzies on campus. They rarely dared to meet fraternities. All she wanted was a nice boy to like her for herself, not just her large breasts, who would take her away from her mother's complaints and her father's disinterest. But the nice boys were scarce, or they were busy elsewhere.

She frequently forgot her loneliness by wandering along Fifth Avenue, looking in the expensive shop windows, imagining a husband who would shower her with gifts. The day after a disappointing twenty-first birthday, with no classes scheduled, she went for a walk on Fifth Avenue. She was looking in a shop window, when in the reflection she saw the boy from the library. He walked by very quickly and before she could even turn around, he was lost in the crowd. She thought sadly of their brief meeting, turned to go, and saw him walking slowly and casually towards her.

"Well, hello," he said.

She smiled and put a pleased look on her face. "Hello."

"Do you remember me?"

"Of course. You're the boy from the library."

"That's right. C16."

They laughed together at this. They stood in the swirl and rush of lunchtime city people and their smiles began to strain as they searched for words. Finally he blurted, "Are you in a hurry?"

"No. I'm just going shopping. Why?"

"Did you have lunch yet?"

"Yes."

"Have coffee with me?"

"That would be nice."

"What's your name?"

"Rhoda. Rhoda Haskins. What's yours?"

"Allen Ross. Glad to know you, Rhoda."

"I'm glad to know you, Allen."

They got acquainted over coffee, somehow surviving their nervous gropings at conversation back and forth long enough for Allen to invite her to the party. No one was really very interested in them at the party, but the many introductions made Rhoda feel affectionate toward him. She held his arm constantly and danced close to him. It was the first time that socializing, not sex, was expected of her. Allen was delighted that he wasn't alone and more delighted by Rhoda's obvious pleasure. It was a very satisfactory evening. Allen took Rhoda home, kissed her goodnight, and went home feeling cheerful. Rhoda was ecstatic. Her passport had arrived. He had made another date before he left.

Their courtship was ordinary. Allen thought mostly about sex and not being alone. Rhoda thought about marriage and not being alone. It worked well for both of them. They went to movies; secret agent films for him, subtitles and happy endings for her. They tried a Broadway musical and they liked it. They went to a football game, but she didn't understand it and he didn't like the crowds. They took long walks and as the nights grew colder, shorter walks, ending in the semi-finished basement of Rhoda's house, where they kissed and touched, sometimes a little more, but not much, until the voice of Rhoda's mother echoed downstairs, sending him home, each time too soon.

Time brought them swiftly together. Time and too much shyness and yearning. They saw each other on weekends. Thanksgiving dinner was at her house. He got a raise; a nightclub to celebrate. At Christmas they gave each other bracelets; hers ankle, his wrist. New Year's Eve they went to a nightclub. Later that night, at her house, half naked, her parents came home early, thwarting his lust. Four months went by. When the school semester ended, they saw each other every night. He was always urgent when they were together. She was urgent when they were apart. School started again. She came to meet him after work, sometimes sitting through his classes. They sent each other sentimental cards: "Be my Valentine." Then one evening his landlady was away, she seeming shy, he posing assured, both nervous, later saying it was good. Then spring arrived, bursting them open with hungers. He surprised her by moving to a new apartment and asking her to live with him. She surprised him by saying that it wouldn't be right. So he had to make a choice, and it was marriage.

(Leaving those unlovely chambers of matrimony, how many couples, joined for moments or longer. Waiting the in-betweens away. Remembering the faces of others. License held in twitching hand. Now you didn't forget the ring. I told them where it was. I hope they won't be late. Torrents of discomfort pouring through people. Weak grins. Awkward pauses. Splendor never discovered. Posed in solemn vestments, a stranger, mumbling an instant, ancient rhythms, splashed upon them without meaning.)

The day was a stubborn memory of winter, whipping a cold, sullen wind, reluctant to depart. Rhoda, nose reddened and running, Allen paler than illness, arrived at City Hall, sent there by his father, who didn't want complications. Her mother didn't want an unbeautiful bride. He was bewildered and embarrassed and she hadn't emerged from resentment at her mother, as they wandered through the maze of administration.

"There must be a sign around here, somewhere," he said.

"Why don't you ask somebody?" she snapped.

"And listen to some stupid joke? We can find it by ourselves."

"We've been walking for ten minutes. Ask that guard. Or shall I?"

"No. I'll do it. Pardon me, sir. Where is . . . Where's the license bureau?"

"What kinda license do you want? We got hunting licenses, cabaret licenses, drivers licenses . . ."

"Oh, Allen," she said in exasperation, then turned to the guard. "We want to get married."

"Well, if you go outside and turn left, you'll see a big building with arches. That's the Municipal Building, the place you want."

He stood there grinning at Allen's discomfort, as Rhoda led him away.

"Thank you," she called back.

"You're welcome, lady. Good luck." And when they were almost at the door, he called, still grinning, "Don't forget to turn in your learner's permit."

Allen turned to Rhoda, slightly confused: "Are we supposed to have a permit?"

"Don't be silly. He's teasing you. Now hurry up."

After wandering upstairs and through musty corridors they found the right office. Their parents were already there, standing separately. The introductions were awkward. They showed birth certificates and the doctor's notes to a clerk, paid for the license and were told to wait until the papers were ready. Rhoda didn't mind waiting. She gushed to her father and mother about how she would decorate Allen's apartment. She wanted them to know how happy she was. Neither of them listened very carefully. Her father was thinking of his imitation green-leather armchair. Her mother was preparing a farewell address to her daughter that would properly conclude her parental obligation.

Allen's father had taken part of the afternoon off to attend his son's wedding. He also wanted to bury the tiny shreds of guilt that had lingered after his son left home. He had absolutely nothing to say, as father and son stood together, one wanting the ceremony over so he could return to work and entertainment after work; the other hoping for a few words of comfort, or at least an expression of interest. They all waited in separate cubicles, becoming more restless as other names were called. Finally they heard the last public mention of their separate names and they proceeded to new identities.

(Rooms of visitation. Reeking of the fearful smells of courtrooms. Till death do us part. How many deaths do part before death. What reason? What hunger breeds the visitation? Joined without hope to endure. Come together alone, urging togetherness. Repeating the journeys of others, through corridors that bear no echoes of passing. Speaking no protest at unready joinings, the ponderous binding. I pronounce you unvenereal, and born, and able to pay the fee. Leave here united, man and wife. Go into tomorrow.)

Again they had to wait. This time in a large room that seemed more suitable for criminal trials. The papers were given to another clerk, who said that the magistrate would be ready for them soon. They sat on a bench, in the large room of empty benches, as if they were to be called to the stand, accused of dreadful crimes. Rhoda was finally silent, brooding about his lack of enthusiasm. Her father was yearning for his armchair. Her mother was trying to decide if tears would be a good ending to her speech. Allen's father stared out the window at nothing, constantly tugging at his slightly soiled sleeve to see his wristwatch.

Allen was thinking of other people's reasons for marriage. These were new thoughts, for he always thought people married because they wanted to. But a family scene in the other room had birthed new implications. There was a young, almost unbelievably beautiful boy, perhaps seventeen years old, sitting alone with the pathos of a doomed angel. Two sets of parents and a mildly pretty, slightly bulging girl of about twenty-three, carried on a bitter argument about what was obviously being solved by their appearance together. The boy ignored everything, sitting like an innocent snared animal, awaiting destruction. Allen was rapidly learning that some of the jokes about marriage were true.

The benches did not get softer and time did not pass faster. Their restless squirmings did not distract the clerk from his papers; that veteran of so many squirmings. Conversation had completely deserted them and they sat a group of strangers, each wondering why they were there, hoping it would soon be over. Trips to the toilet for the gentlemen and fresh lipstick for the ladies didn't really help relieve the tension. They all sighed with relief when a door opened behind them and the right name was called at last.

"Mr. Ross?"

The voice belonged to the magistrate, an anonymous figure in black. When they turned towards the sound, he beckoned to them, repeating the name: "Mr. Ross. Would you bring your party into my chambers?"

The not very cheerful party went into the tiny one-room chambers. The magistrate stationed himself behind a desk, flanked by the American and New York State flags. He mumbled good afternoon without introducing himself and went about his preparations, which consisted of opening a worn book to the proper page, then setting a timer that would have been more appropriate for boiling eggs. This done, with a brief, unwarming smile, he turned to the business at hand.

"Well now, young man. If you'll just step up to the desk with the little lady on your left, we'll make this as painless as possible. Will this be a single or double ring ceremony?"

The last impediment dealt with, he proceeded to unite them in matrimony in record time. Barely pausing for responses, he finished and offered indifferent congratulations in well under three minutes. He shut off the timer before the bell rang and waited for them to leave. Bewildered, they left on mechanical legs that took them to the street. They were now joined forever, or as long as forever would last, without the faintest idea what to do next. Then Allen did the most decisive thing in his life. He turned to Rhoda. "Let's say goodbye to our parents and go home."

"Yes, dear," she responded demurely, which they did, to the enduring frustration of her mother, who didn't get to deliver her farewell address.

SOCIAL AGITATION

Billy was sitting curled up in a chair, his twelve-year-old mind trying to make sense of a pamphlet that a striking worker at the supermarket had given him. His mother's strident voice yanked him out of his reverie.

"Go to the supermarket around the corner and get me a broom."

"I can't, Ma. The workers are on strike there."

"So what? I just need a broom."

"I can get it at the hardware store. There's no strike there."

"I don't care about the strike. Those men should be working, not hanging around the streets causing trouble. I heard they had a fight yesterday, right in front of the store. That's disgraceful."

Billy had been hanging around the strikers, fascinated by their actions, running errands, fetching coffee and refusing the money they offered to pay him for his efforts. He tried to explain what they were doing. "The bosses brought in scabs who tried to cross the picket line. The men were sticking up for their rights."

"Where did you learn that disgusting word, scabs?"

"From the strikers."

"I don't want you hanging around with those bums."

"They're not bums, Ma," he protested indignantly. "They're honest workers standing up to the bosses, who want to exploit them."

"What're they teaching you, to be some kind of communist or something?"

"No, Ma. I'm just learning about the labor movement and how they're always oppressed by the bosses."

"You keep talking like that and you'll end up in jail."

"Yes, Ma," he mimicked.

"And don't 'Yes, Ma,' me, mister smarty-pants. You still need someone to wipe your nose."

"Is that all, Ma? Can I go now?"

"Here's the money. Don't spend the change on those crazy books you're always reading. And come back today. I need that broom."

"Yes, Ma."

As he left, he heard her muttering something about "crazy kids these days."

THE EPIDEMIC OF '53

The ride itself was not a long one, two hours at the most. But such significance was attached to it in later years that it seemed to Billy as if a caravan journey from ancient Tyre to the land of Hind would have been more brief. Searing August held the land in thrall. The man-mites coursed the burning pavements and the tar-pit streets in a weary plod, searching for oasis-like relief from the torpid, scorching day. The hospital orderlies grunted inarticulate curses at the sun, the heavy, awkward stretcher that grew heavier by the minute, and their miserable fate at having to work, instead of being able to join the mass city exodus to one of the weekend pleasure spots of the weary toilers, the beach. They kept up a constant clamor about the delights they were missing at the fabled seashore.

The very word *beach*, to the unenlightened, conjures up an image of deep blue, tropical waters, rolling rhythmically upon a white sandy shore. But Coney Island was nothing like this serene image. Visited by the empty beer-can scattering tribe of man, Coney Island was an arena of delight for ten thousand devils, fiendishly gloating over the tortures inflicted daily on all who were foolish enough to enter this arena of torment. First the bold adventurers ran the gambit of the boardwalk, bounded on one side by food stands selling all the viands that clog arteries: cotton-candy, hot-dogs, french-fries, soft-drinks, beer, and ice-cream. On the other side there was a rusting iron fence overlooking the beach, with an occasional pay telescope for the convenience of the optically challenged to peer at the bathing-suited maidens without having to venture into the fray.

Next, visitors descend a flight of stairs leading to the beach, pausing to shed their shoes before they became filled with coarse, grating sand. Then they pursue a course designed to leave them as close as possible to the inviting water, followed by the indignant shrieks of outlying fragments of the dense mass, unappreciative of possessions and persons being trod upon by sand-burned feet, echoing behind them. Finally, the spreading of the blanket, disrobing, racing across the hot sand and plunging into icy water, splashing around briefly, then coming out to lie on a blanket atop gritty sand containing the discarded refuse of ten thousand fellow sufferers. Then broiling in the baking sun until it's time to return to hot, uncomfortable homes. And this was what our faithful bearers, unhappy with their princely burden, yearned for.

They had deposited the frightened boy on a traveling stretcher, in the hearse-like ambulance. Billy thought of the many times he had seen similar vehicles racing through the city streets, siren wailing, carrying someone to the hands of crisp, efficient doctors, who he imagined would coolly mend battered and broken frames. With the feeling that this shouldn't be happening to him, and still finding it difficult to accept that he had the dreaded disease, he carefully watched the orderlies for any clue to his condition.

The ambulance drove along the waterfront section of the Belt Parkway, through the drab greyness of one of the many tenement neighborhoods of Brooklyn. Trapped on the uncomfortable traveling stretcher, Billy craned his neck so that he could see the ancient, rusty freighters loading their mysterious cargo that would go to strange, exotic ports of the earth. Then they raced through the tiled smoothness of the Battery Tunnel, with the faint pressure beneath the river pressing on his ears and the exhaust stench of the noxious engine fumes filling his nose and throat with a stinging touch that made his eyes water.

Finally, after feeling that sunlight was forever lost, they came out of the tunnel and Billy saw the large sign advertising gasoline that greets the jaded traveler entering Manhattan. Then up the cobblestoned ramp, with Billy breathing a silent prayer to beat the automobile racing alongside his once ambulance, now racing car.

Urging his heroic driver to go faster, despite the risk, then accepting defeat as the high-powered car of his opponent, Crash Kelly, roared past with a dangerous burst of speed.

Billy found consolation looking at the great, sleek ocean liners, snugly secured to vast wharfs jutting out on the dark flow of the Hudson River. On the far side of the river, the unknown land of New Jersey was gaudily bedecked with huge billboards and neon signs, blatantly attracting attention to the virtues of their products. Tall water, gasoline and oil towers stood awkwardly on craggy cliffs, surrounded by grim factories and warehouses. In the distance, there was the magical allurement of an amusement park, whose wonders and delights had never been tasted.

On the New York side of the river, Billy watched with yearning eyes when he saw the fast-moving bodies of young boys playing ball in the parks that bordered the highway, each of them separated by ordered swatches of green. His mother spoke, breaking the revery of remembered games. "The rehabilitation hospital is supposed to be very nice." *How could a hospital be nice?* he thought, nodding vaguely. His mother retreated into her own thoughts again. He tried to think of something to say indicating interest, but was distracted when he saw the George Washington Bridge connecting them to the unknown world growing larger, as the ambulance sped on.

They went through a series of sharp turns, then entered the access road leading across the vast, shiny structure. Billy looked down at the water and saw small boats chugging up and down river. Their remoteness, due to the height from which he was looking, made each boat seem like a tiny realm inhabited by sprite-like creatures. The ambulance paused as the driver paid the toll, then they continued on the road, with turnoffs leading to turnpikes, thruways, and highways, each one preferable, but the driver, with malicious cunning, found the road that led to the hospital, where Billy would spend the next year of his stolen youth.

As they drove on, Billy stared with avid hunger at the boys seen momentarily in the small towns they passed, running and playing with abandon. This brought images of himself and all the games and activities of his childhood, inexorably vanished with the coming of polio. He watched the trees bordering the road with their leaves turned yellow by the hot, pulsing sun. When the clouds occasionally parted, he could see the deep, flowing tides of the Hudson River, making his past life seem distant and strange. Higher and higher they climbed, as the road went into the Catskill Mountains and he looked upon the vastness of the unknown land and fear was born; the peculiar fear that comes when one first painfully learns that the carefree, unthinking time of youth is forever lost.

They passed a faceless small town and the driver, in venomous perversity, remarked, "We're just about there." Then the boy knew that this was no tortured nightmare, with salvation imminent by awakening. He began to accept the full significance of his condition for the first time; he was paralyzed.

The ambulance turned across the highway and went up a steep, narrow road bounded by slopes of seared grass. He saw a drab, grey-and-white columned building that looked like a shabby plantation in the movies. They passed a blur of low, red-bricked buildings that all looked the same. They stopped by the building which he knew would be his home. His stretcher was wheeled up a ramp, through a door to the ward nurse's office, then into a temporary isolation room, where he was placed on a bed.

His mother, with affectionate and tender words, said farewell, promising to visit as soon as possible. The boy saw the anguish and unspeakable torment in his mother's eyes, but was too young to understand that affliction is a searing pain to those who love the afflicted one. So he watched her go, unaware of her isolated anguish during the long, silent ride back to the city, unaware of her impotent and frustrating vigils to come in the stillness of long, sleepless nights, and unaware of the agony brought about by the crippling of the child of her flesh. And the boy felt the first dagger-thrust of aloneness that would bind him adamantly for the rest of his life.

The New York State Adaption Institute is located north of New York City, upon a hill that overlooks the Hudson River. It sits on the ancient site of one of the many battles George Washington lost in the Revolutionary War. The institute consists of red-bricked buildings with green-tiled roofs that had a factory-like efficient appearance, shaped roughly in a quadrangle, with outcroppings of buildings including a laundry, resident personnel dormitories, and others whose mystery was never penetrated. The buildings were surrounded by neat but scraggly grass patches, giving the entire area the appearance of a sterile, small town college, where the local progressive citizenry might send their barely functional offspring to incubate and not embarrass the family.

The buildings in the quadrangle comprised the working area of the institute that the patients had contact with. They included two main ward buildings; one for male patients, with one floor for those over sixteen years of age, called the "men's ward," and the other floor for those below sixteen, called the "boy's ward." The building for female patients was similarly arranged.

Once he was left alone, he lay there on the bed petrified and silent. His mouth was dry in an agony of fright. The doctors had said that he would never walk again. The words burned through his brain in hot, unbelievable flames that consumed all his courage, all his strength. It was just a few days ago, running down the street with his friend Tommy, never knowing that it would be the last wild use of limbs that so soon belonged to someone else, or should. He didn't want to recognize that he was the immobile body concealed under the covers, already taking on the look of the imprisoned. He stared from captive wounded eyes, asking the same question over and over: "Why me?"

Darkness fell, bringing the first hospital night for the boy. Lights suddenly flared, throwing grotesque, hovering shadows on the bile-green walls. The scuffing footsteps of nurses in the hallway brought him memories of recent summer nights and the distant whispers of unknown strangers, passing in the darkness. Nurse Wheeler, the night ward nurse who he would get to know well and who had grown dismal from the sufferings that each night brought, stopped at the door of the isolation room. "And how do we feel tonight?" she mumbled, then hurried on without waiting for an answer. And the night slowly passed and he lay alone with his new unmoving body as the hours crept by, and he struggled to endure the fearful, sleepless watch. And when no sleep came no dreams came and he was trapped in his inert flesh with no hope of escape.

He remembered the terrible events of the last two weeks that brought him here. He had been working as a junior counselor in a day camp in Brooklyn. He was fifteen years old and it was the first job that gave him responsibility over others, and he was thriving on it. He had worked as a bicycle delivery boy at the age of eleven, getting up each morning at five a.m. to deliver the Brooklyn Eagle to its enlightened readership. He had been the youngest and smallest delivery boy, suddenly introduced to the carnivorous world of work, bullied and harassed, until he learned how to deal with his peers. Two years later the demise of the Eagle ended his ride. When he was fourteen, a neighbor got him a job in the mail room of Warwick and Legler, a politically connected law firm, that included John Foster Dulles as a senior partner, a powerful player in Republican circles. Billy was politically ignorant and didn't grasp the stature of the firm and no one bothered to educate him. So the summer passed in mechanical chores performed by rote, although he learned how to interact with sophisticated adults.

In the summer of '53 he was strong, fit, and full of juices. He had joined the high school gym team the year before as a sophomore and had blossomed physically. He was a shade under six feet, with curly brown hair and intense brown eyes that hungrily probed everything around him. He had a striking rather than a handsome face, a persona that instantly attracted friends and enemies, and a growing confidence in his abilities. By the second day of camp he had established himself by the assured way he did whatever was asked of him. He was treated the same way as the older counselors, the college boys, and despite their difference in years, felt the equal of some and superior to most. By the end of the first week he was flirting with three girls, the youngest of whom was seventeen, and he had a short, but exciting sexual encounter with a girl of twenty-two.

For the first time in his life Billy was happy. He came from a poor family, with a harsh father who took out his failures and frustrations on his son. Only recently had he become strong enough to put an end to the oppressive beatings that had gone on since early childhood. Now his father still cursed and yelled at him, but it was a minor annoyance compared to regular violent attacks. His father never struck his mother, but she had been worn down by his endless verbal assaults. He had hated his mother for not protecting him when he was a child, but he finally recognized her inability to deal with the ugliness of confrontation and now felt sorry for her. He was doing well in school, getting good marks, and he had actually made some friends. He had a series of girlfriends, several of whom significantly added to his sexual education. He started to believe that there might be a tomorrow for him, up to the day he got sick.

He hadn't noticed anything physically significant in the second week of July, not even a fever that didn't debilitate him. He went to work, tended the kids, flirted with the girl counselors, and was really enjoying himself. He came home one day and his mother remarked that his face seemed flushed. She felt his forehead and told him he was burning up. He felt all right and started to go out for the evening, but she insisted he see the doctor. She phoned the family physician, Doctor Pearlman, who had taken care of their family for years. He urged her to bring Billy to his office immediately. The country was in the midst of a polio epidemic that was terrifying people everywhere, particularly in the big cities. When Dr. Pearlman made a preliminary diagnosis of polio, Billy thought he was joking. "Are you trying to scare me?" he asked scornfully. "I feel fine." But it was no joke. The doctor sent for an ambulance that took Billy to Kingston Hospital and an isolation room.

Despite the doctor's assertion and the contagious warnings on the doors, Billy still felt fine. After lying on his bed for two hours with nothing to do, he got restless and went for a walk. When he got back, the nurses, doctors, and administrators were frantic and screamed at him to get back into bed. He began to understand how lepers felt. They put him in restraints and gave him a spinal tap, an agonizing experience, that confirmed he had polio. When he woke up in the morning, he was completely paralyzed from neck to feet. He didn't believe it at first. Only when he tried to move and couldn't, did the horrifying reality begin to sink in. He had no idea what to do or think, so he retreated to that inner place that let him endure his father's beatings. The doctors were pleased to tell him that morning that he would never walk again. He couldn't believe that they could say something like that and his "Fuck you. I will," was not received cordially. But he didn't care and vowed that he would walk again, no matter how long it took. The doctors spitefully told him that as soon as he was no longer contagious he would be transferred to a rehabilitation hospital, somewhere in upstate New York.

So here he was at five thirty a.m., trapped in his bed, when Nurse Harmon, the ward nurse who he would later come to detest for her callous, frigid indifference to the patients, brought in the juice cart. There was a limited choice: concentrated orange, tomato, or grapefruit, in tiny cans dripping with early morning sweat. "Do you always bring juice this early?" he asked.

Nurse Harmon stared at him coldly and ignored his question. "Orange, tomato, or grapefruit?" she asked implacably.

"Orange, please." Their eyes locked and the roots of conflict were born. "You didn't answer me. Why do we have to get up so early?"

She glared at him, hands on hips. "It's ward policy. Are you going to give me trouble?"

He managed to bite back a smart-ass retort. "No. What happens after juice?"

"We wait until breakfast."

"When is that?"

"Seven thirty," she answered, looking at him challengingly. He didn't respond, beginning to realize that he was trapped in an alien world, with unknown rules.

The wait until breakfast felt interminable. He started to doze off several times, but each time Nurse Harmon appeared, as if by remote control, and stridently said, "No sleeping before breakfast."

"Is there something I have to do?" he asked reasonably.

"No."

"Then why can't I sleep?"

"Ward policy. Do you have a problem with that?"

He decided not to argue with her until he knew more about the place. "What happens after breakfast?"

She stared at him for a moment, then answered in a monotone: "Toilet and personal hygiene at eight. School from eight thirty to noon. Lunch at twelve thirty. Physical therapy from one thirty to two thirty. Hydro therapy from three to four. Occupational therapy from four thirty to five fifteen. Dinner at five thirty. Ward lights out at nine on the boy's ward, where you'll be moved after dinner. Questions?"

"I can't move. How can I do those things?"

"This is a rehabilitation hospital," she explained scornfully. "We'll help you."

"Oh."

The only palatable part of breakfast was the ward attendant who fed him. She was a local girl, who in another section of the country would have been a hillbilly. She had stringy brown hair, a pale face, washed out blue eyes, but a ripe body that swelled in the appropriate places. The corn flakes were pasty, the milk watery, the breakfast roll stale, the butter tasteless, but her hand that casually stroked him as she fed him with her other hand, made him forget what passed for a meal.

"What's your name?" she asked nasally.

"Billy. What's yours?"

"Lizzie Jo. But you can call me Liz." And while they talked her hand kept wandering his body and he didn't know what to do or say. "This your first day?" she asked, while her hand asked something else.

"Yeah. What kind of place is this?"

"It's a hospital for paralyzed people."

"I know. I mean what's it like?"

"You'll find out," she answered with a giggle. "I've got other patients to feed. See ya." And off she went, leaving him trying to figure out what she was up to.

The rest of his first day at the hospital was as strange as breakfast and passed in a blur. The school teachers treated their physically dysfunctional students as if they were mentally challenged. The level of classroom work was designed for the retarded and that's how it was presented. He didn't say anything as he tried to understand what was going on. His unmoving body was shuttled from therapy to therapy. At physical therapy, Stan, a short, stocky, extremely hairy man, seemed to take pleasure in stretching Billy's limbs until he screamed in pain. Then he explained how it was for his own good. By the end of the day Billy was so exhausted that he had no objections when the lights went out for the night. He lay there in the darkness feeling the shame of being processed like a piece of meat, with as much consideration for his sensibilities. Just before he fell asleep, he vowed to himself that he would deal with this nightmare and someday walk again.

THE HOUSE IN THE STOVE

It has always been cold. We never could afford a stove, so we tried to keep warm wearing the leavings of one hundred strangers. But if we never quite succeeded in losing the chill that made our fingers stiff and clumsy, there were times when life was rich and full. One of these times was when I was five years old. A man knocked on the door. My mother opened the door and asked what he wanted. He said that he represented the welfare agency of the city, and that our name had been given to them in order to provide us with assistance. At this, my father, who was listening from the bedroom, mustered the little dignity that remained to him and said, "Sir, I have made many mistakes in my life, but I have never permitted myself the degradation of accepting charity." He returned to the bedroom with the haunting thoughts of pride and his children, who were never warm.

The man turned to go and then he noticed me. "Are you cold, son?" He lifted me and placed me on his knee. "I'm going to tell you a story," he said. "Once there was a family who lived in a great big black stove. They ate coal and wood, and drank kerosene. Sometimes they were hungry, but generally they had enough to eat. One day, though, there was a great noise and the stove shook and fell on its side. After that it was carried away somewhere and dropped with a terrible thump. The family was very frightened. Soon they began to grow hungry. They waited for a long time, becoming hungrier and hungrier, when suddenly the door to the stove opened and someone gave them food." At this point he looked at his watch, muttered something, put on his coat and said, "I'll have to finish the story another time," and went out the door.

Three months later I contracted pneumonia. The doctor told Mommy that I was going to die. My brother Jimmy came to see me and told me that when I died they would put me in an oven. Then I could live in a stove and be warm, just like in the story.

THE AUDITION

"Next," the stage manager called. I looked around to be sure it was my turn, and she repeated impatiently: "Next." I took a deep breath, put on my combat face, stood up, and walked to center stage, struggling each step of the way to control my nervous trembling. Only the work lights were on, so I could clearly see the people running the cattle call. There were five of them. Why did they need five? Could this be one of those democratic collectives, where everyone argued instead of working? The stage manager handed what I assumed was my resume and head shot to who I assumed was the director. He briefly scanned it, then passed it on to the others.

I waited until the last person was finished reading and comparing me to the picture, trying to appear cool and confident. The director had been looking me up and down, lingering a moment too long on my breasts, which I resented, even though I should have been used to the unwanted attention by now. "Sing," he said.

I looked at him in surprise. "I was told that I only had to prepare a monologue," I said.

He ignored my feeble protest and said, "Sing."

"What kind of song would you like?"

"Anything."

I took a deep breath and sang the first two lines of "Greensleeves." I thought I was pretty clever,

since I was auditioning for a Shakespeare play and it might impress the inquisition panel. A lot of good it did. They stared at me blankly.

"Dance a beautiful dance," he ordered.

"I'm not a dancer. I'm an actress."

Once again he ignored my objection. "Dance a beautiful dance."

I briefly considered telling him to shove it, but I hadn't done Shakespeare since college and I had learned that there were very few opportunities. So I did a beautiful dance. At least I thought so. It was some kind of cross between a waltz and a fox trot. It was the best I could do. There was no reaction from the inquisitors and I was beginning to get pissed off. If they wanted a prima ballerina they should have said so in the actor's call in the trade papers. Part of me wanted to walk out without saying a word, but another part wanted to do the show. Besides, I didn't want to give the assholes the satisfaction of watching me slink off, tail in the traditional place, another defeated actor.

By now I knew that something unexpected would be next on the menu, so I smiled pleasantly at the inquisitors. I got a quick rush of pleasure when some of them looked surprised. After all, it was obvious by now that they were trying to freak out the auditioners. They probably assumed by this time that the auditioners would be agitated and in the process of losing their stage persona. I had no idea why they devised this torture session. It was different from any audition process I had been through. Maybe they had already cast the show and were getting their rocks off by torturing some needy actors. Stranger things happened in theater. Whatever. I was here and I certainly wasn't going to break down for their viewing pleasure.

The director gestured to the stage manager, who handed me a sheet of paper. It was in French. The director said: "Read." I knew what he would say if I told him I couldn't read French, so I read. Maybe Charles Baudelaire would have objected strenuously about my pronunciation, if he was there, but I was beginning to enjoy myself.

"That's enough," the director said, staring at me expectantly. I guess he was waiting for me to ask how I did. I just stood there silently. He looked me up and down, again lingering too long on my breasts. "We'll call you." I just nodded and left. I knew they would call. I had seen that lecherous look before. Now it would be up to me to decide whether or not to do the show. Part of me was hungry for Shakespeare, but these were weird people. I wasn't sure if I was up for any more bullshit in my life. Then I laughed. I didn't have to worry about it until I got the call.

MISSPENT

John Richardson, a tall, weathered, handsome man, lost to passing time and stares of hungry curiosity, sat on a small wooden bench as the snow hurled taunting tastes of cold tears in the small garden, part of a posh building that he had carved himself apart to possess. He had sacrificed his integrity for the pomp and security of a fine address, the servile respect of doormen, elevator operators, and employees who had reason to visit his home. Yes he had hungered for the things bought with money, but he had allowed that hunger to mold him, had let desire give birth to ambition and more desire.

He softly said aloud, "I remember when I was nineteen years old, struggling through college, dreaming of fine restaurants, owning Picassos, a seasonal box at the opera, the pleasures and visions of the grand life, the beauties of man's creation. But also the lost dream of great things; God how I wanted to paint, show the world the beauty and torment that raged through me like a mad storm, howling and roaring, never letting me rest."

The overpowering façade of the giant luxury apartment house towered over the small surrounding garden, making the Homburged gentleman seem puny and futile. He sat, lost in a world of sorrow, as snow flew, covering his black coat and hat with white flakes. He was as intense as brooding sculpture, shoes buried by somnolent flakes, face blanched by cold and pain, silk scarf whiter than purity, shining between the black stretches of hat and coat.

The passing swarms of city dwellers rushing home from work, rushing home to shelter, rushing . . . rushing . . . rushing . . . paused before the glass and steel elegance, sentried by a snow splattered lord of the city, sitting as still and forgotten as an ice age relic, and spent one brief curious moment wondering about the distinguished man, sitting alone in the snow on a garden bench, before forgetting him a moment later, as they continued on their way home.

FEARFUL FLIRTATION

I couldn't help staring at him whenever I thought he wasn't looking in my direction. He was handsome, well-built, probably tall (I couldn't be sure, because he was sitting), with dark hair, pale skin and a sculpted face with intense dark eyes that attracted me, even though I only glimpsed them momentarily. I wasn't sure of the pick-up protocol at the Borders coffee shop, but my usual fears of meeting strange men were already kicking in: AIDS, date rape, miscellaneous forms of abuse. It must have been a lot easier in the Sixties, when guys didn't give you a fatal disease, or kill you when you said no.

One of my girl friends at New York University told me about Borders. She said that she met some nice guys there. I was a fairly good-looking young woman, tall, shapely, athletic, with short blond hair, blue eyes, and I was always well-dressed. My problem was that I was burdened with large breasts. I knew why that brought undeserved attention from the wrong kind of men; low-lifes had been coming on to me since I was fourteen. But there should have been nice guys out there with only two hands, who were willing to look past my breasts at the real me. I just hadn't been very lucky.

A succession of bad relationships had turned me into a nervous doe, ready to flee at the slightest sign of aggression, and there were always signs. My last relationship had become really ugly and the seemingly nice guy quickly became a monster, hitting me when I wouldn't do what he wanted. After I broke off with him he stalked me for weeks. I lived in constant dread that he would do something terrible to me. He finally evaporated, but I still had trouble sleeping and kept trying to grow eyes in the back of my head. I wasn't ready for a lesbian relationship, though NYU seemed to specialize in extracurricular opportunities. I was a little out of step with many of my classmates. I really wanted a man.

I sensed him looking at me and felt a flush warm my body. I sneaked a peek and yes, he was staring at my breasts. As we made eye contact, he shifted position so I could see the bulge of his crotch. He was hot, no doubt of that, but he was too aggressive for me. Did he think I would respond just because he spread his legs? I would, if I dared. But I was too afraid of what else he might be offering. I slipped on my coat, picked up my books, and fled, a panicky animal urgent to escape the hunter. Maybe there was a safe way to meet a nice guy, but I hadn't found it. If I couldn't get my nerve up to ask around the dorm and face the sisters' scorn, I had run out of other options. I just had to decide which was worse; being an object of ridicule, or being lonely.

HIPPIE BREVIS

Was it not said of old that you shall be men who hold your heads proudly and walk in peace and love? (He rolled over on his side, moaning drunkenly in oblivious imagery of last night's bacchanal.) Was it not said that you shall people the earth and produce many sons who would go forth with fecundity as kin? (His whiskered, unwashed body of aloneness turned in troubled whimpers to his pillow of forgetfulness and lay barren.) Was it not said that you shall know truth? (There was light. He awoke and with the first anguished awareness tried to return to stupor. The voice of his household God summoned him into existence with a harsh, insistent ringing. He obeyed and arose.)

He put on crumpled shorts, an old torn sweater, dirty Levi's, battered moccasins, doused his face with cold water, dried it, briefly contemplated and rejected breakfast, and went out. (The air was cold. It was good and pure, but he knew it not. He was a poet who lived in an attic in lower Manhattan. He thought he suffered to know life, although this was never admitted to anyone and rarely to himself. He spent his nights drinking and his days in frenzied conversations with his artistic friends, who like himself suffered for art. These are the prophets of beauty.)

Pretty Lilah was at home. "How about some breakfast?" he said. "I haven't eaten since Tuesday." After listening to an entertaining lie about the guy who bought them drinks last night, she fed him.

He has a brilliant mind, she thought. *Why doesn't he stop this nonsense and get down to work?* Once every two or three months this brilliant mind wrote six or seven lines of what was considered poetry by his advanced group. The minor event served as a topic of discussion for another month. (Where is the poet of this age who shall know wisdom and compassion, perhaps beauty?)

They went to the coffee shop where their friends gathered. Here life was explained; never lived, but explained. A long red beard called an invitation that was accepted without haste. They slouched in low quaint, atmospheric chairs and ordered espresso. "What did you do last night after the orgy broke up?" asked the beard. He did the talking. She was silent, for she was deep. "Man. I just about swam home. Like I was wet." The beard pondered and relapsed into silence. They called it Zen. (O Patriarchs of the doctrine forgive them.) Others floated into the circle, contributed sundry information and disappeared.

He gestured to pretty Lilah and they left. "Everyone's gone today. They're just not there," he said. She said nothing and he continued: "Well I'm getting sick of this town. As soon as I get some money I'm going to Europe. To hell with America and all the money-grubbers. I want to be somewhere where I can breathe and not have to smell someone worrying about feeding his children, or paying the rent. It gets me sick." (On and on unto an eternity of lies and petty stupidities that will comfort the being of emptiness, until the mystic day of revelation comes, bringing forth the buds of truth that will flower and turn to weed.)

"Let's go to your place and talk." She silently acquiesced. They climbed five flights, opened a rotting door, lit a gas lamp, and sat down on a musty studio couch. He babbled to her, while contorting himself to edge closer to her. Then he awkwardly kissed her and she dutifully responded. He made hesitant, clumsy love to her for a while and, because of the ignorance of youth, stopped, lit a cigarette, and resumed the impalpable discourse. (Where is the man who shall reach for the woman and find satisfaction in the act of togetherness? Not in the youth who know only presumptuousness.)

And so the time passed. He left and on the way home picked up a bottle. Sweet serum of drowsiness taken each night to assure a tomorrow that shall be as many yesterdays, until there is rest. Poet of an ideal, carry the flaming banner of art, until it shall scorch your greedy hands, but suffer bravely and never learn that life contains enough suffering and makes unnecessary worship of the god pain.

GIRL TALK

Mavis Carver and her new best friend, Jennifer Van Meer, had finished their calculus homework and temporarily exhausted the topic of their costumes for the Halloween Ball and the exciting young men who would swarm them. They were relaxing for a few minutes before Jennifer had to go home. Mavis remembered how they recently met at the introductory dinner for Dr. Carver, given by the other department heads to welcome his official appointment as head of cardiology. Mavis was used to important social functions, but she had never been to such a high-powered event. Medical department heads in the distressed condition of America now ranked almost as high as the heavy hitters of the military-industrial complex and politicians. Although she didn't understand all the nuances of her dad's new position, Mavis knew enough to realize that he was now a man of importance. She also knew that her behavior would reflect on him, so she was very careful to behave properly.

She had bowed to everyone she met, according to rank and station. Dozens of faces set in formal expressions blurred during the ritual of bow and smile, except Jennifer's. Her mischievous look was fleeting, but her wink was unmistakable. Mavis had to fight for self-control, or she might have burst into laughter, which would have profoundly offended Jennifer's father, Doctor Van Meer, the influential head of virology. He had an air of self-importance that hinted he wouldn't appreciate Mavis's frivolity.

Later, Mavis had a moment alone with Jennifer and took her to task. "What did you think you were doing, girl? I almost laughed in your father's face."

"But you didn't. I wanted to find out right away if you were the right kind of material."

"What do you mean?"

"I needed to know if you were an upwardly mobile, capable American woman. I don't have time for ward scrubbers." One part of Mavis verged on anger at Jennifer's blunt, elitist attitude, but the other part liked her refreshing directness and that part won out.

The two girls became as close as sisters, confiding almost all their secrets to each other. They quickly built an alliance that strengthened them in the lofty political world their fathers moved in. Jennifer was sixteen, only a year older than Mavis, but she seemed much more mature. She had bright red hair, green eyes, and a deceptively plain face that was lit up by the energy of her dynamic character. She was tall and slim, with a runner's body, a contrast to Mavis's light-skinned, strong African-American features and a lithe dancer's body. She was quite bright, although not as smart as Mavis, but unlike Mavis, she had a life plan. She was going to be a doctor, predetermined by her roots and training. She had already decided that she would be a radiologist, since she would be able to control her work schedule. This would allow her time to fulfill her agenda of acquiring a suitable doctor husband and conceiving two doctor-to-be children. She was appalled by Mavis's casual attitude to the future. "You have to get with it, kid," she urged Mavis. "This isn't the old days, when there was time to find yourself. The world's a difficult place for Americans now and I want the best life I can get. I strenuously suggest that you should want the same good things for yourself. We could become very important people some day and help each other."

Mavis didn't really disagree with Jennifer's way of thinking, she just resisted out of stubbornness. When she confessed that she still harbored fantasies of being a modern ballet dancer, Jennifer tried to give her a quick dose of reality. "That would have been fine in the Nineties, kid, when everybody wanted to be some kind of artist. These days, the arts don't play a very prominent role in America.

The only work you'd probably get would be at one of those strip clubs, where you'd have to suck off the customers."

"Ooky . . . Have you ever been to one of those places?"

"No, silly. But I've heard some of the interns describe them. Believe me, it's not for you."

"But I love to dance. I can't give that up."

"Fine. Take a class whenever you can, but don't forget your priorities. You can't let dance interfere with your preparations for medical school. Once your career is on track, you can give small performances for a select audience, if you feel like it."

"You're right. You're so sensible, Jen. I really appreciate that. I guess it's med school."

"Among your many fine qualities, kid, you're smart. It's a tough world these days. You just have to grow up faster than you'd like.

CURTAIN CALL

Just as I reached for my makeup case I remembered that I forgot to replace the red blood cake that I needed for Act III. I turned to Milton, the youngest actor after myself, who had appointed himself my mentor when I first joined the company.

"Milt. Can I borrow some red cake?"

He shook his head in mild rebuke.

"Will you ever learn to always take care of your basics? How do you expect to succeed on stage if you're not prepared?"

I suppressed a laugh of derision. I knew the future of the company was doubtful at best, even if the old timers refused to admit it. Milton, in his mid-fifties, was still considered a youngster by the rest of the company, all of whom were in their sixties. But he had been helpful from the beginning, following my audition six years ago, at the age of thirty-five. So I listened politely to his usual lecture, then thanked him for lending me his makeup.

It wasn't his fault that I had made a disastrous choice of working in live theater, instead of film or TV, which every practical actor was doing. How was I to know that live performing arts would disappear almost overnight? At first I didn't notice when opera went because of diminishing audiences and rising production costs. I didn't like ballet which was next, followed by classical music. I wondered if all those longhairs would be playing rock or country. It was no surprise that Broadway musical theater producers held out the longest. After all, musicals were the most accessible of the performing arts. The producers blamed the unions for their failure, claiming extravagant salaries and benefits that made production impossible. But nobody believed them. It wasn't labor's fault, or even greedy producers. The audiences were gone.

I still found it hard to believe that an aging population, with reduced incomes, preferred to watch large screen TV, rather than performances, even though they couldn't compete with film's sophisticated technology. Theater's more primitive efforts in trying to be hi-tech couldn't compare to dazzling cinema computer effects, and audiences were no longer very excited by new musicals, many of which sounded alike. I guess the only reason museums survived was that visitors could zip through quickly, take some photos, then be on their way after a short, painless dose of culture.

So why didn't I have my head examined before I chose live theater? Because I loved it and I was too dumb to recognize that its day was over. As my company's audiences got smaller and smaller, their unenthusiastic heads got greyer and greyer. I had started a lottery to guess the age of the youngest member of the audience by the color of their hair. This outraged the sensibilities of my fellow performers, whose original hair color was long past its heyday. But we were doing it a few weeks later and Milton was the first winner, picking a full crop of black hair on a well-preserved fifty-year-old.

Our biggest problem, besides our looming demise, was play selection that our dwindling subscription audience would accept. They were adamantly opposed to young love, romantic comedy, high tragedy, social issues, or anything emotionally disturbing. This eliminated most of the classics, so we did a lot of Moliere, Restoration comedy, and this season we were daringly presenting Shakespeare's Julius Caesar, our current production. As the youngest male, I was typecast as Marc Antony and I had actually noticed a few nods that might have been approval for my performance among the dozing heads. I didn't expect much more. We were not getting the love from our audience that actors crave.

I don't know what I'll do when the company folds. Gretchen, the venerable artistic director, who always babbled about the struggles of Stanislavski during the Russian Revolution, promised us one more season. I doubt that. For the last two weeks we had very small houses at every performance, even Saturday nights, less than half a house, once the height of choice of theater goers' excursions. I'm probably too old, at forty-one, to break into any meaningful TV roles. I don't even have an agent. I don't have any marketable skills, not even bartending. My only shot at making a living on TV would be doing commercials, if I had an agent. If I got jobs.

I'll probably spend the rest of my life as a waiter, as long as there are half decent restaurants, and I'm fit enough to carry a tray. I can't blame anyone for my poor career choice, so I'll do the best I can to survive. And I must confess, even though I don't dare say it to the rest of the company, I still get a thrill going on stage, even if the audience doesn't.

IN THE GARDEN TROD A REBEL

"Jeez, lady. Dem puppies is cute. Are dey dem Peekin geese dogs?"

"Leave Twinkle and Twither alone," she snapped frostily. "Can't one walk in Central Park without being bothered by you trash?"

"I was just gonna pet dem, lady. You don't hafta get mad. I likes little dogs. I wouldn't hurt 'em."

"Go away before I call that policeman."

"Aw c'mon, lady. I didn't do nuttin."

"Are you going, or shall I call him?"

"Awright, awright. I'm goin'. I didn't mean nuttin. I'm not botherin' nobody . . ."

"Hey, you bum. Quit botherin' the lady," a passing man said.

"I'm goin'. I'm goin'."

"Well hurry up, or I'll help you along with my foot."

"Da whole world's always helping me with its foot, I ain't gonna take it no more . . . You see?" And he pulled a knife from his pocket.

"Now put that knife away . . . Don't get excited," the man said soothingly.

"I ain't excited, and I'll calm down, as soon as I put my knife away. In you . . . Like dis."

"Oww!" the man yelled in pain.

"Help, help," the woman screamed.

The policeman rushed over. "What is it, lady?"

"Oh, officer," she said and pointed. "He stabbed that man who was only trying to help me."

"I better put the cuffs on you. Hold out your hands," the policeman ordered.

"I didn't want to stab him," the man explained. "I don't know how it happened, but he said he was gonna kick me and all of a sudden he was like the whole world kicking me . . . He, that lady with her puppies, and all the stinking people in Central Park . . . Jeez, I guess dey really got me now . . . Yeah, I guess dey got me good."

JOURNEY

Centuries ago, a great prince traveled from China to India and brought a famed Taoist magician to divert him. Each night when the tents were set up, the Taoist went to the prince and told him strange and wondrous tales of the heroes of Han, The Three Kingdoms, and Tang. The prince listened respectfully and graciously thanked the Taoist for the benefit of his wise tales, but was still so bored that his spirit fled to the ninth heaven and he feared for his life. One night, he wrapped a simple robe about himself and wandered around the camp, until he reached the fire of the herd-boys. Four boys, fifteen or sixteen years old, were bragging to each other of the adventures they would have when they reached their destination. The prince sat quietly in the shadows and listened to the boys talk.

One said: "I will gorge on all the new and delicious foods and strong wines of this strange land." Another said: "I will lie with many women who are comely and rich, and I will please them so much that they will buy all manner of jewels and costly garments for me." The others laughed, because they knew he was not bold enough to dare accost a foreign woman. A third said: "I will learn the use of weapons from a great master and when we return home I will become a great war-lord and have much power." The fourth youth sat silently, staring at the fading embers, and occasionally tossed clods of dung on the dying fire. The three youths taunted him and one said: "What will you do, Erh-Lang, sit and listen to Priest's prattle?" "Oh, no," said another one. "He thinks he'll find a great teacher and become an immortal." "No, no," the third one insisted. "He'll find someone to show him the way to the Jade Emperor's heaven, so he can beg for the elixir of life."

Erh-Lang smiled at the three boys, whose teasing hadn't the least bit annoyed him. "All I will do is look at the new places that are strange and wonderful, and talk to the people I meet in this foreign land. If I am lucky, I will learn a lot and go home a little wiser than before." The other boys laughed and jeered. "You are a fool," cried one. Another taunted: "You are a peasant, and that's all you'll ever be." The third said: "You have no ambition and will get nothing in this life." Erh-Lang shrugged. "I will get whatever fortune grants me and enjoy a lot or a little, whichever may come." The three boys sneered at him. Then they went back to their boastings, ignoring their self-contained companion.

The prince had been listening in fascination to the boys' conversation and looked carefully at each boy so he would remember them. Just before they broke camp in the morning he summoned the boys and asked each of them the same question: "What will you do when we get to India?" The glutton answered fearfully: "I will serve you, highness." The lustful one quavered: "I will serve you, highness." The bully stuttered nervously: "I will serve you, highness." When it was Erh-Lang's turn, he said respectfully, but confidently: "I will learn all I can about this land." The prince nodded approvingly. "Good. You will accompany me as my servant, while I learn about this foreign land. The rest of you will remain herd boys, because you are too foolish to recognize your friend's superior ability."

THE ICEMAN

Christopher Herter guessed it was a typical early December lunchtime crowd at the Bryant Park ice skating rink, mostly tourists, shoppers, and the occasional nearby office escapee. He waited with the others behind the rail for the Zamboni to complete its last circuit and for the next session to begin. He cursed under his breath in disgust, still fuming at recently being banned from the Rockefeller Center rink, for what they called offensive behavior. In a scene of mortifying humiliation, the manager had announced over the public-address system that the ushers were to alert him immediately if Chris ever reappeared. The manager also blared that he would have Chris banned from the Wollman rink in Central Park and other rinks in the city. All the regulars watched avidly as the police escorted him out, which insured that they wouldn't be inviting him to their parties anymore. This was particularly galling, since it meant the end of free meals and cut off a social setting where he sometimes collected an unwary woman, a newcomer to skating circles, unused to encountering an extremely cunning sexual predator, who could be deceptively charming.

With his constant attitude of never being in the wrong, Chris refused to admit to himself that he was to blame for the incident that had resulted in his banishment. After all, how was he supposed to know the girl was only thirteen? She looked like she was at least eighteen or nineteen. When she told him she was a college student he had no reason to doubt her. It had started as it always did. He was displaying himself in the center of the rink, doing jumps and spins, attracting attention to his verve and skill. He was in his early thirties, a bit over six feet, with dark curly hair and dark eyes, set off by his pale skin. His taut, muscular body was outlined in a tight, formfitting white turtleneck and snug black pants. He peripherally observed the girl admiring him and after briefly assessing the other skaters, he selected her as the optimum choice of the day.

He prepared her with his usual thoroughness. First he verified that she was definitely interested, then he made sure she was watching when he executed a particularly dynamic move. After several brief eye exchanges, he flashed a low-medium wattage smile that caught her attention and provoked a smile in response. He skated to her and the rest was a matter of technique. "My name's Chris. What's yours?"

"Lottie."

"That's a nice name. I never heard of it before."

"I was named for a German opera singer," she replied nervously. He was used to that. She was young, lush and ripe for the picking.

He confidently put his arm around her waist and said, "Let's skate." As they glided around the oval he was just beginning to explore her body when someone abruptly yanked his arm, pulling him off balance.

He started to turn and swing at the intruder, but confronted a big, red faced, angry older man, who yelled loudly, "Take your filthy hands off my daughter." The rest was inevitable.

So here he was, exiled from the land of milk and honey, reduced to scavenging in a lesser arena that in the three days he had been going there had been completely unproductive, adding to his feelings of disgrace and frustration. He doubted that the manager at the Rockefeller Center rink could actually get him banned from other rinks, but that didn't make him feel any better. His appetites, normally kept under rigid control until he could exercise them, were becoming increasingly urgent. It wasn't that he wanted to hurt women, he just needed the thrill of their fear and pain for his own arousal and fulfillment. So he indulged in rough sex. So he gave them a few scrapes and bruises. So what? He didn't do any real damage and he provided a unique learning experience. He only used them once and never bothered them again, so no lasting harm was done. He even took perverse pride in thinking they would never forget him.

Aah. He rolled the bitter pill of scorn under his tongue and half-heartedly scanned the skaters as they made their way onto the ice. Whoa. His eyes clicked like a raptor on a young woman who stumbled out of the gate and desperately clung to the railing, as she tried to make her feet do what they were reluctant to do. He looked her over closely. She was short, slightly plump, but curved in the right places, with blond hair and a roseate complexion. She looked corn fed, straight out of the farm and susceptible to the nice-guy-trying-to-be-helpful act. He watched her hobble around the rink twice before he concluded that she was alone, then begrudgingly decided that there were no other candidates and selected a reassuring, non-threatening approach.

He timed his arrival just as she stumbled, easily accomplished since that was all she was doing. "Hold on there, miss. I've got you." And he carefully took her arm, steadying her. He used a low-wattage, sincere smile, meant to generate trust. "With just a little help you'll be zipping around the ice easily."

She blushed and said with a laugh, "I'm afraid not. My feet slip rather than zip on ice." And she giggled at her attempt at wit.

"I wasn't doing much better than you a few weeks ago," he offered. "Then this nice older lady helped me around the rink and gave me some pointers. Now I'm really enjoying the ice." He gave her his most sincere I-am-a-trustworthy-fellow look and urged gently, "Why don't you give it a try?"

"I don't want to bother you."

"It's no bother. It's my way of repaying a kindness." He extended his arm and she slowly took it.

"Now stop whenever I become a burden," she insisted.

"Don't worry about it. Just enjoy yourself and learn to skate."

Chris assisted her courteously, making sure that he didn't reveal any appearance other than the skating Samaritan. They made their way around the rink slowly and she gradually relaxed and actually began to skate.

"I don't believe it," she gushed. "I'm really skating."

He gave her another low-wattage, manly forthright smile. "You're not quite ready to do a figure eight yet, but with a few small adjustments you could skate by yourself and decide if you like it. Would you like me to help you?"

"Oh, yes. If it's not too much trouble. I don't want you to give up your skating time."

"There's plenty of time for me to skate and in just a few minutes you'll be off on your own."

"You're very nice. Thank you."

He showed her how to control her balance and movements, handling her very respectfully, and after a few minutes she stopped worrying about falling or looking foolish. He quickly caught and supported her when she stumbled, making sure he didn't touch her in any way that might be considered intrusive. And lo and behold, in just a short time she was skating on her own. Her eyes shone and her face was flushed with excitement. "This is wonderful. You're a great teacher."

"Not really," he replied, projecting modesty. "You're a good athlete. I just helped a little."

"Yeah. Right. You don't know how clumsy I am."

This time he offered a medium-wattage smile, designed to make her realize how attractive he was. "I think with a bit more self-confidence and some practice you could do a lot of things that you were afraid to try." He injected a small hint of suggestiveness. "You look like a very capable young woman." She flushed and didn't respond, but he knew she got the message.

A pang of annoyance stabbed through him, part from wanting to possess her, part from resentment that she was just an ordinary country mouse, not scoring very high on the desirable scale, and bitterest thought of all: right now she was the best he could do. He masked all signs of violent emotion that if perceived would send her scurrying for safety. He watchfully escorted her several times around the oval, noting the rapid improvement in her ability to skate freely. She gave him frequent looks of *How am I doing?*, seeking approval from the handsome stranger who had unexpectedly befriended her. She was really beginning to have fun, when a PA announcement said, "In a salute to the past, the next session will be for couples only. The regular session will resume in ten minutes. Thank you."

Skaters began to make their way off the ice and the girl turned to Chris with a pouty look. "Darn. I was just starting to do well. I'll probably forget everything by the time I get on the ice again."

Chris shook his head and smiled at her sympathetically. "You won't forget. You're doing fine. A lot of guys would be glad to skate couples with you."

He coldly watched her gather her courage, then she asked shyly, "Would you?" She was so pathetically easy that he almost said no, but a quick survey of the rink convinced him that there were no better prospects. The tension he was so scrupulously concealing reminded him that he needed to vent his built-up frustrations, and at the moment she was probably the best that an exile from Rockefeller Center could find.

Chris flashed a medium-high wattage smile and showed her the position they would skate in. Once he had his arm around her he leaned closer, adding another level to her awareness of him. "Since we're suddenly so close, it's time for introductions. I'm Chris." He could feel the heat emanating from her body wherever he was touching her—arm, back, hip, leg—and he made sure she felt his heat, all the while presenting a courteous façade that was disarming. She was blushing non-stop and he could see that she was already beginning to fantasize about a romantic encounter.

"I'm Maryann. It's nice to meet you."

"It's my pleasure, Miss Maryann," he addressed her on an impulse, and smirked to himself as she devoured what seemed like good manners. He figuratively patted himself on the back for being clever enough not to have shown off his skating skill at the Bryant Park rink, which might have drawn the wrong kind of attention. After all, he hadn't decided whether to come back here, or go somewhere else.

He took masterful control of her and she let herself be swept away in his arms, completely oblivious to his voracious appetite lurking just beneath the surface. The feeling of his body moving against her produced tingles of excitement in her that were alien to her sensibilities. Her last titillation had been in anticipating her first open-mouthed kiss, which didn't live up to expectations. After that, sex had been more of a peer-group obligation, rather that the burning passions of chick-lit books, or the steamy joinings of R-rated movies. It wasn't that she didn't have desires. It was more like the boys she met just didn't turn her on. The three boyfriends she had experimented with had ranged from limp, to sweaty, to clumsy, and in their different ways had left her sexually tense and remote. She was a little afraid of the stirrings she was feeling for Chris, but so far he was a perfect gentleman.

By the time the couples' session ended, Chris knew that Maryann was ripe for the plucking. This made him despise her for being so trusting and he became angrier, although he camouflaged it even more thoroughly with surface charm. He saw that she was slightly fatigued from the unaccustomed exercise and had been sufficiently exposed to stimulating physical contact. He politely took her arm and guided her off the ice. "I don't think you should overdo it the first time out. Why don't you sit down for a few and I'll get you a hot chocolate." He led her to a nearby table, held her chair as she sat, then said, "I'll only be a minute. Then I'll say goodbye and you can decide whether or not you want to skate anymore." He walked away before she could respond, but he was certain that she was hooked and wouldn't let him go.

The hot chocolate affected her almost as much as if it had been an aphrodisiac. She showed all the symptoms of infatuation: doting glances, flushed cheeks, rapid breathing, and she babbled away like mad. All he had to do was nod encouragingly as she gushed about her home in Cedar Rapids, Iowa, the family tradition of working in a furniture factory, and playing in the local symphony orchestra. Music was apparently the only way for her family to express individuality, because she described how each one played a different instrument. He listened attentively as she described her studies at the state agricultural school where she was a junior, preparing for a career as a veterinarian. He silently nicknamed her *Doctor Bovina*, and had to catch himself before he snickered derisively. She finally wound down a bit and said, "Here I've been running on about myself and you've just sat there like the strong, silent type. Tell me about yourself. Where are you from? What do you do? Who is this prince charming who rescued me?"

He instantly decided to tell her as intriguing a tale as possible and smiled modestly. "I'm no prince charming. I'm just a struggling artist. My father was a diplomat and I was born in Paris. We moved every few years, mostly to African countries, but sometimes Japan, or China. My mom died when I was two, so I don't remember her. I went to American schools wherever we were stationed, but they were different from the schools back in the States, more sheltered from the harsh realities of life. Dad wanted me to follow in his footsteps, but diplomacy wasn't for me. When I decided to go to art school in California he disowned me and we haven't spoken since. A gallery in LA started showing my work a few years ago and actually sold a few paintings, so I took a chance and came to New York. I'm getting some paintings ready so I can try to find a gallery to represent me here. Until then, I'm just another starving artist. That's it. That's my story." He didn't even have to look at her to know she believed every word.

"What an exciting life," she enthused. "Not like my drab existence."

"It's not as interesting as all that. It's been a real struggle to survive on my own and paint, hoping that someday I'll be a known artist, with my work in museums." He stared wistfully across the park, as if gazing into the future at his paintings hanging on a wall in the Whitney Museum, looking past the leafless, sickly sycamore trees and not seeing the graceless Grace building across 42nd Street.

"How can you say that?" she demanded mock indignantly. "You've been everywhere, seen everything, and you're making it on your own. This is my first time out of Iowa and except for meeting you, it's been like I had my nose pressed against a restaurant window, watching people eat while I was starving. The only person I talked to in the last two days was the desk clerk at the hotel. I actually stopped someone on the street and asked directions, just to hear another voice."

He knew, as he always did, that the moment had come. He stood up slowly. "I didn't mean to monopolize your time. I'll just say goodbye and leave you to your skating."

"You can't go," she blurted, then tried to cover up her growing fascination with him. "You launched my career as a skater and now you want to abandon me? How about you skate with me for a little while longer, then I'll buy you dinner as a way of repaying you for what's become a real fun trip."

He gave her the medium-low wattage, too-proud-to-accept-charity smile. "I'll be glad to skate with you for a while, but I couldn't accept dinner."

"Why not?"

"I wouldn't want to take advantage of your generous nature."

"That's silly," she said. "I've been taking advantage of you. It's the least I can do."

He emitted the medium wattage sweet smile. "I'll skate with you and we'll see about dinner later."

"No. It's settled." He shrugged helplessly, then led her to the ice.

Maryann was having the time of her life. She was still feeling the aftereffects of being alone in the fabled city, and she transferred all her emotions to the good-looking guy who came out of nowhere and had transformed her vacation from empty to full. She kept glancing at him as they skated, fervently hoping he wouldn't disappear as suddenly as he had arrived. "Could we skate as a couple again?" she asked shyly. "It really helped me before."

"Sure." His arm slipped around her and she immediately felt a wave of pleasure engulf her, followed by unaccustomed surges of desire for the hard, masculine body that held her so securely. She lost track of time as they went 'round and 'round and noticed nothing else but the man beside her, wishing that these delicious moments would never end.

When the PA system announced the end of the session and requested the skaters to leave the ice so it could be cleaned, Chris was disgusted with himself for wasting so much energy on a dumb rube. Without the challenge of winning someone over and enforcing his will on the victim, there was no thrill of conquest. His greatest satisfaction had come when he humbled a haughty ice princess, reducing her formerly unobtainable body to a quivering mass, as she pleaded with him not to hurt her anymore. It wasn't the infliction of pain that aroused him. It was the burning sensation of power, while he compelled a woman who was used to being in charge to obey him. He looked Maryann over once more and concluded she wasn't worth the effort. He decided to return the rental skates that cost eight dollars and seventy-five cents, grumbling to himself mentally for not bringing his own skates, then dump this dreary girl before she really angered him.

He headed for the exit, not even bothering to say goodbye, then he heard her calling him: "Chris. Chris. Wait for me."

He didn't want to be remembered by anyone, so he suppressed his impulse to strike her and turned with an abashed smile. "I didn't want to obligate you," he said softly.

"You're not getting away from me that easily," she asserted. "I insist on taking you to dinner."

He felt a surge of rage, but he masked it, not wanting to attract attention. "That's very nice of you, but I don't want to impose. Besides, I need a shower. I'll get one at my studio and call you later."

"I can go with you. I'd love to see your paintings."

He thought quickly. "My studio is way out in Brooklyn and I share it with another artist. We're not allowed to bring anyone there."

Then she had the most daring impulse of her life. "You can shower at my hotel."

He mentally gritted his teeth, beginning to regret that he had tried to spare her. "Let's go," he said, and offered her his arm.

They walked north on the Avenue of the Americas, both lost in their own thoughts, hers much gentler than his, until they passed Radio City Music Hall. "I always wanted to see the Rockettes," she said. "Did you ever see them?"

"No," he muttered, aggravated further by her sweet simplicity. A few minutes later they reached her hotel, a non-descript pile of brick and concrete without any redeeming architectural value.

The doorman nodded politely and opened the door for them. As they passed through the lobby, the desk clerk called "Good afternoon, Ms. Jensen," and Maryann cheerfully replied "Hi, there."

Chris knew that if he did anything to her he might be identified later, so when they got to the elevator he said coldly, "I can't do this. I've got to go." He turned and walked away, and behind him he heard her start to cry. His last thought about her as he obliterated her from his mind was that she'd never know how lucky she was that she had only shed tears, rather than blood.

FADED HOPES

Jimmy and Stella Vann lived in a ratty old tenement building on Canal Street, serenaded by the clomp and shove of daily shoppers and the spastic traffic roar of Holland Tunnel nights. Their weekdays were divided with Jimmy pushing carts in the garment center, a diminishing industry that was dissolving as fast as the rest of American industry was evaporating. While Stella sewed sequined dresses for young Hispanic brides, in a sweatshop loft on West 27th Street that always smelled of dead rats.

But the weekends were their days of rest. On Friday, after work, Jimmy and Stella would go shopping in a Chinese grocery that was part of the expansion of Chinatown in every direction, spurred by a dynamic population explosion. It never occurred to Jimmy or Stella to speculate if Chinese reproduction could keep pace with the Mexican illegal immigration in the coming struggle for lebensraum in America. They would buy food and beverages for the week, then go home and Stella would cook dinner, while Jimmy watched TV. After they finished eating, Stella would wash the dishes and Jimmy would dry, a chore they enjoyed doing together.

Dinner was a nutritional task that came before indulging in the night's pleasure, drinking beer. They both had an extremely low tolerance for alcohol, so they quickly achieved a numbing high that allowed them to forget their slave-like labor of the week. Jimmy and Stella never had extensive dreams. They met at a party in a local bar and fell into sort of liking each other. They experienced neither burning passion, nor wild ecstasy, merely a tolerant accommodation that allowed them to avoid complete loneliness and dwell in an illusion of normal existence. They became habituated to each other and gradually lost touch with their few friends and family.

Jimmy's company abruptly off-shored its business to Vietnam. He discovered with a shock that the company hadn't paid its share of unemployment insurance, so he was ineligible for benefits. A week later Stella's sweatshop was raided by the police, who shut the place down for illegal working conditions. Suddenly they were without an income. They tried to cut back on expenses, but finally ran out of money and couldn't pay rent. In the tradition of unconcern by landlords for distressed tenants, they were promptly evicted.

Jimmy and Stella were faced with trying to live on the street, or going to a homeless shelter. They had seen enough of the streets and had heard terrible stories about the homeless system, so the prospects of either were horrifying. Stella, always the more practical of the two, spoke bluntly: "We got more than we expected outta this life. I don't want to live like a bum. Do you?" "No. What do you wanna do?" She looked at him more intently than ever before. "Let's go to the Brooklyn Bridge and end it all."

Jimmy stared at her in amazement. It took him a moment to digest what she said. "You mean jump?" "Yeah." "That's crazy." "Is it?" "Yeah." "You got a better idea, Jimmy?" He thought for a minute. "No . . . but that's killin' ourselves. I don't know if I could do

it . . . I don't think we should do it." "How about we just take a walk to the bridge? If you think of somethin' else we can do on the way, we'll try it. Okay?" "Yeah. That sounds good, Stel. At least it'll give us a choice." "Yeah, Jimmy . . . Let's hold hands the way we usta. That way we'll look like other people for a while." "Sure, Stel. That sounds nice . . . Let's go."

JUNKIE INTERLUDE

They lay there on the grass, lazy and sailing. The man had come, bringing the joy dust, the wonderful white powder that freed them from worry. They didn't have to think about getting sick; the slow horror of the growing need for smack, coursing through the blood, setting muscles twitching, nerves screaming, and every particle of mind shrieking for the sweet peace and contentment of heroin. So they lay there on the summer grass in Tompkins Square Park, cigarettes burning down to their drooping fingers, then falling on their clothing, burning unnoticed holes, until the hot coal of the butt started to sear numbed flesh. Then they would lift slow-motion hands and brush away the smoldering ashes.

The three of them were lying on the sparse grass, unconcerned with where they were, or what was happening around them. Full of the security of having just taken off, and not having to worry about scoring for a few hours, they were as puissant as kings in their own minds. Manuel and Ripper wore short-sleeve shirts, because they skin-popped, hitting themselves in the buttocks with the needle. Hermano, who mainlined, always shooting up the big vein in his forearms, wore a long-sleeved white dress shirt, buttoned at the wrists, to hide the tracks left by a hundred needles.

The daily life of the park swirled around the three supine figures. Old men sitting in the sun on well-worn green benches, people walking dogs, young mothers with children playing in the sandbox, boys playing baseball, young men playing soccer, and a few ancient women gossiping, relics from another land. It was a calm day in the city park that frequently erupted into protest, chaos, and violence.

Manuel, Ripper, and Hermano lay there motionless, without desire. Lying in the hot sun, completely at peace, they wanted nothing but to lie there forever, remain high, and be warmed by the gentle heat. They didn't say much to each other, occasionally opening a languid eye and with a slow effort, lifting a heavy head and mumbling "This is good stuff, huh man?" to which there would be soft words of agreement. So the junkies were at rest. No more sweating for enough money to score. No more fear of getting burned with bad stuff, because they were already sailing from the good smack. They wanted nothing more then lying on the grass, soaring through imaginary worlds, being licked by the tongue of the hot sun.

They fit in naturally in the constricted park environment, because they didn't bother anyone. No one paid them more then a moment's attention, before moving on to more interesting sights then three young men, dozing in the park. No one could know that when their high collapsed, they would lie, steal, assault, and prey on any victim who would provide them with the means of escape from unpalatable reality. No one realized that the three young men in their ignorance supported criminal cartels that eroded the fabric of democracy, with a flood of drugs that poisoned the nation and consumed its treasure. But innocent park goers couldn't be expected to connect these three young men to the forces of evil that plagued our land, on such a beautiful day.

AN ACTOR PREPARES

"Not like that, Andrew," Eliot whined for the fourth time. "You're supposed to be having a nervous breakdown. You have to look it, not just say the lines."

"I'm working on it, Eliot," I replied, in the tone that I knew would piss him off. "I'll get it. It just doesn't come as naturally to some of us as others." And I looked at him suggestively. Eliot glared at me impotently, a look that I was used to, since he resorted to it frequently. We had been at loggerheads from the first day of rehearsal, when I took exception to his request to keep working past the contracted time.

"Eliot," I said in a patronizing tone, "Union regs don't let us rehearse more than six hours a day. This is a showcase. You were told the rules by the union rep. If you like, I'll show you the handbook. I didn't make a fuss when I didn't get all of my allotted break, but it's time to respect Equity rules. You don't want me to file a grievance, do you?" I scornfully dismissed his silly appeal for me to forget the regulations for the sake of the show. That was when he glared for the first time. As if he cared about anything but his dumb concept. Then he babbled to us about the need to work hard to produce art. The other actors nodded solemnly, but I laughed in his face. "This isn't art, Eliot. It's like a meat market with talent for sale. If you want art, you shouldn't be doing a showcase."

I must admit I enjoyed watching him squirm when I reminded him in front of the others that the showcase system was designed primarily to allow actors to demonstrate their talent to agents and producers. I didn't bother pointing out that actors couldn't demonstrate very much with minimal rehearsal and three weeks of performances. But that didn't bother me. I mean it's not as if we're trained like dancers, with all kinds of different skills. I had a different agenda. I wasn't really interested in theater, though I knew I could do the classics if I wanted to. I wanted a career in television. A part in a long running show was my goal, with the accompanying rewards of fame and fortune.

Unlike many actors, I had disciplined myself to put on a good front and always look confident, even when I felt like crapping in my pants. The truth was that I was meant for the showcase system that encouraged surface skills and facility. It was an ideal vehicle for me to display my confidence, relaxed ease, and magnetism. I hoped that by doing showcases I would land an agent and maybe even get a commercial. That would pay my freight as I worked my way up the ladder to a big-time TV show. This was my fourth showcase and nothing had happened yet, but I was still hopeful.

I hadn't bothered explaining the plan to Eliot. He wouldn't see the logic of it. He was another dumb liberal arts grad with a degree in directing. He'd have a better chance for regular work if he became a traffic warden. At least he'd be able to direct motorists, who might listen. He had no real idea what he was doing and his selection of the play further indicated how dumb he was. Nobody would stay awake while a young man had a nervous breakdown in front of his father, mother, and older sister, just because he was turned down by the college of his choice. Well, maybe the playwright's mother. And Eliot didn't even know how to block properly. He kept putting people in front of me, so I couldn't be seen while I was doing my lines.

To make matters worse, Eliot had cast a retired insurance executive as my father, and a retired school teacher as my mother. I never understood what prompted these greyheads to suddenly try a second career in theater. These retreads took everything very seriously and went about their business as if they were preparing for a Broadway opening. They even supported Eliot when he demanded that I learn my lines. I tried to explain that I would know most of them by opening night. They got real nervous when I said it wouldn't make much difference, since the audience didn't know the script, so they wouldn't know if I dropped a line or two. But they kept hassling me. Mr. Insurance Company mumbled over and over: "How will we know our cues, if you don't say your lines?" They freaked out when I said: "Just wing it, pop."

Eliot had cast a slightly overweight, nervous girl as my older sister, but she wasn't bad looking in a fleshy sort of way. I figured to slip her some unbrotherly love, once she got to know me. There was nothing better available. I never seemed to meet anyone at my waiter job at the restaurant, an untrendy hamburger joint, where the female customers kept their legs tightly shut. So I had nowhere else to meet women . . . But sis turned out to be an ingénue, trapped in a bulky body, and I was just too crude for her. Then, as if things weren't bad enough, the playwright showed up and droned on and on about how we were missing the real theme of the play: "The breakdown of high expectations." Give me a break.

Well I can get through two more weeks of rehearsal. Maybe the show won't be as bad as it sounds. And if they give me a hard time, I can always walk. That's the beauty of the showcase system. An actor can leave the show anytime for paid work, or an audition for paid work. And what would these losers do, bring a lawsuit to the union? Fat chance of that. If things go bad and I decide to split, I'll just pick an audition from a trade paper and say I have to prepare for it. But it may not come to that. If I don't have anything better, I'll stick it out. Maybe I'll get lucky this time and I'll get discovered. You never know.

LOSSES

It was my second day on the job and I was still nervous, unsure of what I was doing. I had been on the waiting list for a year to get into the union, Local 50 of the Bakery, Confectionary, Tobacco Workers, and Grain Millers International, the only way I'd be allowed to work in the big Bronx bakery. Now I had my opportunity and I hoped I wouldn't blow it by doing something dumb. I had experience in a small neighborhood bakeshop on Westchester Avenue, but it closed when the landlord raised the rent. The boss let me go and I had been unemployed ever since. Unemployment insurance wasn't enough to pay the bills.

Most of the workers at the factory were at least in their forties or fifties and had been working for the company for a long time. They treated me like I wasn't too bright and I had to take it. I was too new to complain to my shop steward, who insulted me more than anyone else. My wife, Maria, was six months pregnant and I couldn't afford to lose this job. I had been assigned to the cookies division, to monitor a mixer. All I had to do was make sure the ingredients flowed in and the dough flowed out to the ovens. It was so simple that an idiot could do it, but my shift supervisor kept telling me I was doing it wrong and making nasty remarks. I wanted to hit him, but I kept my cool.

I got through the first week, despite the lack of help from my fellow workers. Maria carefully stretched my paycheck for rent, utilities, and a few basics, but we had one nice meal with meat, and for dessert, reject cookies from the factory that weren't good enough for packaging. Things were definitely looking up. We were relieved that we would be able to keep our apartment, pay off some of our debts, and maybe even go out to a club some Saturday night.

But most of all I wanted my daughter to have a home of her own. Then suddenly everything fell apart.

The union had been negotiating with the owners, rich investors from somewhere in Massachusetts or New England, and our representatives told us they would reach a deal. It turned out the union refused to accept cuts in pay and benefits. So the membership voted and on a beautiful August day we went on strike. I was one of the few who voted against walking out and I got plenty of dirty looks, curses, and insults. I had tried to tell them that it's better to make concessions and keep jobs when so many people were out of work and the economy was in trouble, but they shouted me down.

The next day I joined the picket line. Somebody shoved a sign in my hand, "Company unfair to workers," and told me to start walking around the factory. I shuffled around for hours, then took a quick lunch break, peanut butter and grape jelly on white bread sandwiches and coffee, provided by the strike fund. When I finished my shift I went to my representative and explained that I had exhausted my unemployment benefits and had no income. He promised to get me a weekly stipend from the strike fund, but it turned out not to be enough to cover our rent and other living expenses.

We were forced to give up our apartment and move in with Maria's mama, a fine woman who welcomed us gladly. But the place was overcrowded with us and Maria's three younger sisters. I hated being dependent on Maria's family like that, but I had no choice. So I walked the picket line six days a week. And summer changed to fall, then winter, and I trudged through the snow, freezing my butt off. The only consolation was that no one had broken ranks. We all suffered together.

In the spring of a deepening recession, the union sued the company for unfair labor practices. To our surprise we won the case and the right to return to work. Everyone was walking on air. We went back to work, proud that we had beaten the greedy bosses. I started planning to search for an apartment right away. Then we got the shocking notice. The owners decided to shut the factory for good, rather than pay the workers what we had struggled for, for almost a full year. The factory was scheduled to close in ninety days. The owners issued a statement that the workers had no one to blame but themselves, for refusing to accept that the operation could no longer afford the wages and benefits it had provided in better times.

The president of Local 50, a tough talking woman, told the workers, "We weren't asking for big raises. We just wanted to keep what we had." I didn't feel any better knowing that now we'd get nothing. She reassured us that the union and its lawyers would study the legality of the planned shutdown. She added they'd also try to find a buyer who would continue operating the bakery. Yeah, right. Like someone else would come in and pay us what we wanted.

Maria took it real well when I told her the bad news, and said, "We'll have to save every cent we can for the next three months." What a great girl! I swore to myself to get another job and give her what she deserved.

The next few months were tough for me. Some of the old union people kept telling us we really won a victory. But it didn't feel that way. I couldn't help thinking that if we only made some concessions we'd still have good jobs. I almost punched out one old guy who kept telling me: "We're not beaten. We'll fight them and win again." I wanted to tell him it was one more defeat in the Bronx, but I shut my mouth. All I could do was do my job for the next few months and hope for a better opportunity down the road.

ASSIMILATION

In the early hours of morning, when the city streets deceive with a silent, soft appearance, I happened to be walking through Tompkins Square park, with its usual well-ordered Parks Department sickly sycamore trees, geometrically placed. The park had iron-mesh fences that prevented the neighborhood kids from trampling the sparse grass. Frigid stone benches, designed to afford the utmost in discomfort, were slowly crumbling from abuse and non-maintenance.

As I wandered towards an exit I heard the refrain of a concertina, slowly and methodically pouring out the rhythm of an old Ukrainian peasant song. I saw four people sitting together. There was an old man with the shriveled look of a Caucasian muzhik, but with a lively glint in his eyes, still undimmed by the strangeness of his bewildering land, playing the concertina. Three old women swayed in time to the music, which had a ghostly, far away sound, as if it welled up from the soul of a forgotten time. There was something haunting and entrancing about these old people, drawn together by the binding spell of an almost primitive folk music, in some simple rite of communion.

A woman suddenly lurched into the circle of light, who was so drunk that she could barely manage to walk. Yet she approached them, as if sent from some darker land to join the swaying group.

She sat on a nearby bench and mumbled to herself, her throat pulsing with the beginnings of a powerful invective. Suddenly she yelled, "Ha, you son of a bitch. You think you can dance? I can dance better than you." The man and the other women laughed, not unkindly, as if the challenge wasn't foreign to their earth-bred natures.

Then the woman asked belligerently, "Do you drink?" rolling each word gutturally in the base of her throat. This evoked another bout of laughter from her audience. Then she said, "Well, if you drink, see that you fuck." She made the announcement with a complete absence of the vulgarity that generally accompanies the word. They laughed with her again out of some instantly established bond that had survived a long, frightening sea voyage to the new world.

As I left the park, I looked back for a moment and the woman had joined the others and was passing a bottle around. The last sound I heard was a plaintive song, bubbling from a lost country, a lost society that never gave comfort, but was a familiar sound to the exiles now sitting in the park.

Stories from this collection have appeared the following publications: *The Armchair Aesthete, Hapa Nui, Pens on Fire, Noneuclidian Café Journal, Pequin, Burst Literary Magazine, Double Dare Press, Indite Circle, Laura Hird, Bibliophilos, Skyline Magazine, The Copperfield Review, Dew on the Kudzu, Readshortfiction.com, The Dogwood Journal, Word Riot, ESC Magazine, Scene 360, SP Quill Magazine, The Landing Magazine, Lamoille Lamentation Magazine, Splinterswerve, Better Fiction Magazine, The Cliffs, Crush Magazine, Fiction on the Web, EMuse, The Externalist, The 13th Warrior Review, Writers Muse, Tampa Publishing Co., Clark Street Review, Piker Press, Southern Ocean Review, The Bent Pin Quarterly, Dogmatika, Mississippi Crow Magazine, The Blotter Magazine, Clockwise Cat, Lit Up Magazine, Ascent Aspirations Magazine, Indigo Rising UK, Locust Magazine, LitBits, The Scribbler Ink, Events Quarterly, Blue Fred's Kitchen, Duck & Herring Company, The Subterranean Literary Journal, The Smoking Poet, Page and Spine, The Flash Flood, Istanbul Literary Review, Fiction Press, Kyoto Journal, Cerebral Catalyst, Riverbabble Journal, Shoots and Vines, Alighted Ezine, Short Story, Underground Window, Tom's Voice Magazine, DiddleDog, Volume Magazine, Fiction on the Web, Tuck Magazine, Confused in a Deeper Way, Fey Publishing, Fabula Argentea Magazine, Shoemusic Press, Centum Press, Second Hand Podcast, Chronicle Stories, Fiction Pairing,* and *Sol Magazine.*

ABOUT THE AUTHOR

 Gary Beck has spent most of his adult life as a theater director. He has had numerous published works including *Days of Destruction*, *Expectations*, and his novel, *Call to Valor*, published by Gnome On Pig Productions. Gary has also had several original plays and translations produced off Broadway, in New York City, where he currently resides.

www.ingramcontent.com/pod-product-compliance
Lightning Source LLC
Chambersburg PA
CBHW051953170626
46808CB00007B/2599